PURPLE REIGN

By: Author Barbie Amor

Formally known as Barbie Scott

Thank You To My Cover Model : Vetta @Iamvetta

PURPLE REIGN - TRACKLIST

https://youtube.com/playlist?list=PLKE5pkof98vfyTASwpluqtueMtU4koQPp

Anita Baker "Joy"

Monica "Everything To Me"

Teena Marie's Deja Vu (Been Here Before)

Alicia Keys "A Woman's Worth"

Lisa Fischer "How Can I Ease The Pain"

Aaliyah "I Care 4 U"

Al Green "How Can You Mend A Broken Heart"

Anita Baker "Body And Soul"

Erykah Badu "Next Lifetime"

Jhene Aiko's "Summer 2020"

Michel-le "Something In My Heart"

Prince "Purple Rain"

Reign

"You bring me joy
When I'm down
Oh so much joy
When I lose my way, your love comes smiling on me
I saw your face and then I knew
We would be friends
I was so afraid but your eyes, they'd say, Come to me..."

"Bitch, shut yo' fat ass up, and go get my muthafucking cigarettes!" My mother kicked in my door, screaming.

I smacked my lips while looking at her. It was below thirty degrees, and she expected me to walk to the store to satisfy her craving for a damn cigarette.

"Smack yo' lips again and watch me smack them muthafuckas down yo' throat!" she dared me, running up in my face.

I swear she found any reason to put her hands on me.

Snatching the money out of Angela's hand, I headed over to my closet and began looking through my bucket of shoes. You damn right I called her Angela. She was far from a mother, and I was gonna show y'all exactly why.

"I'm hungry, and it ain't nothing to eat."

"Bitch, keep getting smart."

"How I'm getting smart? I'm hungry."

"Yo' ass better go fix you some noodles."

"Ma, I'm tired of noodles."

"Well, I don't know what the fuck to tell you. Shit, we ain't got shit because yo' fat ass eat a bitch out of a house and home," she fussed, then walked out the room.

I shook my head as I slid into my worn down Adidas that leaned to the side; they even had foil on the tip of the shoe strings so I could lace them up. I grabbed my wind breaker because this was the only jacket I had. You would think with the $500 she got from welfare she would at least buy me a jacket, but nah. That shit went on beer, crack, and scratchers. Just like now. I was starving and hadn't eaten since yesterday, and here it was, she was buying cigarettes. I swear I hated my life.

At seventeen years old, one would think I lived a normal teenage life like most girls my age, but that wasn't the case here. Angela didn't let me do shit. I couldn't have friends, and I could barely go outside. She held me captive because she used me as her personal slave. When I say this bitch didn't do shit but smoke crack; that was all she did. I did the laundry for both of us and even her dirty ass boyfriend. I cooked when we did have food, which was only from the fourth, when she got her stamps, until the twelfth. She got $326, and she sold most of them. For the remainder of the month, I would be eating noodles. Or, I'd be next door at Mr. Gary's house eating whatever he cooked.

Mr. Gary was the old man neighbor who couldn't stand my mama. These walls were so thin, so he could always hear the verbal abuse I had to deal with on a regular. Whenever he would cook, he would sneak me food, and he even gave me a few dollars to get to school.

Mr. Gary had been living next door to us for years, along with his wife, Hatty. Two years ago, Ms. Hatty passed away, so now, it was pretty much just him. Because he was so old, I helped him out around his home as much as I could. He constantly tried to pay me, but I would always decline. I was overly grateful for the things he did for me, and I couldn't see myself taking his money.

"Bring me a scratcher!" Angela yelled just as I was closing the door.

When I stepped outside, I let out a deep sigh and prepared myself for the long walk. The moment I stepped from inside my building, the air smacked me so hard. If I wasn't so big, I prolly would have fallen. I continued up the street to the store. I noticed the same group of guys that always hung on my street in front of my secret friend's, Raylen, home. No matter what the weather was like, they always hung out. I quickly crossed the street, too embarrassed to be seen.

I prayed like hell Katasha wasn't with them. Because anytime I walked by, she would always find something to clown me about. She constantly criticized me about my weight, my hair, my shoes—something. She was one of them boujee bitches who kept herself done up, so anyone with my statue was a joke. She was light-skinned with a long ass weave. She had a body to die for and even a cute face. She knew she was the shit because, not only was she pretty, but she got dough along with the dope boys and drove nice cars. Katasha had it made.

Let me not forget how she messed with who everyone referred to as King of the Streets, Truth. Truth was the nigga who ran the city, literally. Everyone worked for him, and he was the finest nigga that God could have ever created. He stood at least six-feet tall with a body that looked hand-sculptured. He had bronze skin and wore his hair low, cut with waves as deep as the Atlantic Ocean. The nigga also had a smile to die for.

Every bitch in the hood wanted him, and I knew that because Katasha stayed fighting over him. Every other day, she was on the block rumbling with bitches. From the small gossip Raylen and I had shared, he was cheating with a couple broads but respected his relationship with Tasha.

"Fat bitch crossed the street today." I heard Katasha's voice and her little pet monkey on the side of her laughing. I swear I couldn't stand these bitches.

Granted, I was on the plus-side, wearing a size eighteen, but that didn't mean everyone had to refer to me as Fat Ass. I had to deal with the shit from people in my neighborhood, kids at my school, and even my so-called mama. I was so used to everyone chastising my weight that I had become numb to the shit. For some reason, I hated when Katasha made fun of me because she would always do it when everyone was around.

"Man, leave that girl alone." I heard Truth call out as I crossed back across the street.

The moment he said it, the crowd was mute.

The only voice I could hear was Katasha telling him, "What? She is fat."

But I ain't pay it any mind.

By the time I made it to the store, I had to stop and catch my breath. When my second wind kicked in, I continued on into the store and began walking the aisles. I walked over to the section that sold hair products. I bent down like I was looking for something, then slid the bottle of purple cellophane into my titties.

"Y'all ain't got no blonde dye?" I asked to play it off. I needed this dye because the streak I had in the front of my hair was turning back blonde.

"If you don't see it, we don't got it," the Hispanic man, Jose, said, then attended back to the guy standing at the counter.

I headed over to the counter and ordered my mother's cigarettes. As I stood there waiting, my heart dropped because a group of niggas walked in, and Truth was one. He rudely walked up to the counter and slapped his money down, ignoring the fact that I was next.

"Let me get some Backwoods," he told Jose, and Jose immediately grabbed the Backwoods.

I smacked my lips because I was standing here and the nigga just put Truth right in front of me. Once they were done, Jose handed me the cigarettes. I stuffed them into my pocket. When I got outside, Truth was just getting into his car. He looked over in my direction, and our eyes connected. I dropped my head and continued to walk, knowing what he was thinking. *This bitch fat*, or *This bitch ugly*. I mean, what else could he be thinking looking at me?

By the time I made it home, I was frozen. All I wanted at this point was a hot shower so I could warm up. I walked up my stairs and headed into my building. My feet were in so much pain because my shoes were already a bit small, and now, my toes were frozen solid.

"Hey, Reign. You hungry, baby?" Mr. Gary stuck his head out the door just as I was passing by.

"Mr. Gary, you know I stay hungry. What you got for me?" I asked as I walked inside his home.

"Come in here, child, and lock that door. Go wash your hands and make you a bowl. I made spaghetti. The garlic bread in the oven," he said and took his seat right back in front of the television.

He didn't have to tell me twice. I quickly made myself a bowl and began stuffing my face. I tried to eat as fast as I could before Angela came looking for me.

"Slow down, child." Mr. Gary looked over from the TV and laughed.

"I haven't eaten since yesterday."

"Got damn shame." He shook his head.

It wasn't no use in criticizing Angela because we both

knew how she was. I continued to eat, and when I was done, I washed out my bowl and headed into the living room to make sure Mr. Gary was straight.

"Mr. Gary, you good? You need anything?"

"Nah, baby, I'm fine. You run on along before that witch comes looking for you," he said, and we both laughed.

"Okay. I'll be by to—" I went to say before we were interrupted by banging at the door. I looked at Mr. Gary with wide eyes nervously. I opened the door, and Angela stood on the other side. As soon as I unlocked the screen door…

Wham!

I grabbed my stinging face, and tears instantly began to run down my face.

"Bitch, what I tell you about being in this man's house?"

"She was only getting something to eat because yo' trifling ass won't cook."

"Nigga, ain't nobody ask you shit, and I don't need you cooking for *my* fucking daughter!" she yelled at Mr. Gary. "Now get yo' fat ass in the house, fast ass hoe."

"She ain't nothing like yo' nasty dick-sucking ass," Mr. Gary shot just as my mother slammed his door shut.

I stormed into my house, still holding my face. When I noticed Greg, my mom's boyfriend, on the couch, I frowned up and went straight to my room. I knew this shit wasn't over, and I would have to hear her mouth some more. My mother was one of those people who just couldn't shut up. She always had to get the last word, and every word that came out her mouth was harsh.

"I keep telling that bitch stay the fuck from over there!" I could hear my mother yelling.

"She prolly fucking him," Greg added his dirty, nasty ass two cents.

"Bitch bet not be fucking nobody. She give up that pussy

hoe gon' be selling that shit for me."

I lay in my bed just listening to my mother and her dirty ass boyfriend discuss me like I wasn't in the next room. I climbed into my bed, and like I did just about every night, I cried. I swear this couldn't be how I would spend the rest of my life. I hated my mother to the point I hated living. So many times I thought of just killing myself, and the only thing that would change my mind was the faith I held for me turning eighteen. I had one year left, and I couldn't wait. I didn't know where the hell I was gonna go, but anywhere but here was fine with me. I knew it sounded ungrateful, because I have a roof over my head, but I couldn't help how I felt.

I looked at my purple stained curtains and began to sing the first song that came to my mind. Singing was my therapy, and it helped ease my mind. Every night, I would cry and sing until I fell asleep; tonight was no different. I let Monica's words take me to a peaceful place.

"You're everything to me, heey
The air that I breathe, oh
I sigh so I see, oh Lord
You're everything to me..."

Reign

"Reignnn!"

I jumped out of my sleep at the sound of my mother's voice. I rubbed my eyes to adjust them before lifting out the bed. When I looked at my clock, it was only 7:16 in the morning, which made me frown. I didn't have school because it was Sunday, and here it was, she was already at it.

Sliding my feet into my rundown purple teddy slippers, I headed into the living room where my mother always slept. She never slept in her bedroom, and I was sure it was because of the filth. Her room looked like a damn dump yard. The living room I kept clean and because she didn't allow me in her room. Her shit stayed messy.

"Hand me the remote!" she shouted the minute I was in her presence.

I looked from her to the remote that was on the love seat only a few feet away from her. *I swear this bitch lazy*, I thought as I grabbed the remote and tossed it over to her.

"You ain't gotta throw the shit!" she shot towards my back.

I kept walking because not only was I still salty about last night, but it was too damn early for her shit.

As I walked back towards my room, I bumped right into Greg. He stood there smiling with his missing side tooth like shit was funny. When he looked down and looked back up to me, he made me look down at what he was looking at. My face instantly frowned when I noticed his dick standing straight up in his dingy ass pajama pants, which looked like they hadn't been washed since he bought them.

"You a sick muthafucka." I shook my head and walked past him.

"Shit, you fucking old man Gary. You might as well let me hit that sweet pussy," he said, making sure my mother hadn't heard him.

Greg always gave me these crazy ass looks like he wanted to rip my clothes off me. The last time he made a pass at me, I told Angela, and all the bitch had to say was, *"Bitch, don't nobody want yo' fat ass."* After that, I stopped telling her shit and made sure to keep my distance from him. Whenever I came home and she wasn't here, I'd go right back out the door. I refused to stay home alone with him.

When I got back into my room, I closed my door and made sure to lock it. I lay in my bed and tried my hardest to go back to sleep. It was like the minute I closed my eyes, a sudden knocking at my window made me jump up. I walked over to my window and pulled back my curtain. I let out a soft sigh because I knew now that it was over for me going back to sleep. I slid my window up quietly, so Angela wouldn't hear me, and stuck my head out.

"Bitch, what you doing?"

"Lying down. This bitch, Angela, woke me up out my sleep for some stupid shit."

"That ain't nothing new. You can't come outside?"

"No. Shit, I ain't got a good alibi, and she gon' be here all day."

"Damn, man. Some of everybody outside today, and you know I don't fuck with these bitches," Raylen said, then looked off into the air. She pursed her lips as if she were contemplating, but there wasn't shit I could do.

Angela wasn't going anywhere today because she was broke, and not to mention, Greg was here. Every time she stepped foot out that door, it was either to go look for Greg or get her crack.

"Man, make up something."

"Okay, you got a dollar?"

"A dollar?" she asked puzzled.

"Yeah. I can lie and say I'm going to get bread."

"Oh." Raylen reached into her pocket. She pulled out a single dollar and handed it to me.

"Give me, like, twenty minutes," I told her and closed the window shut.

I pulled my curtain back and headed into the bathroom to wash my face and brush my teeth. I also changed into something different so I wouldn't be seen in yesterday's clothing. I knew Ray wanted to be in the front, and all the dope boys were about six stoops down.

"I'm going to the store to get some bread," I told Angela as I stepped into her view.

"Where the fuck you get some money from?"

"I dug some change from the bottom of my backpack, and I had a quarter left from your change."

"Gone, but if I catch you next door, I'mma beat yo' ass."

I flew out the door before she changed her mind. When I stepped off the porch, Raylen was standing to the side hiding. I looked her over and took in her appearance. She had on a black hooded sweatshirt and some pajama pants. However, her hair was laid to the gods, and her eyelashes enhanced her face. Raylen was a really pretty girl, and I couldn't understand for the life of me why she chose me to be her friend. Although Angela didn't allow me to have friends, nothing could stand in the way of the bond we formed.

Raylen kept me on my toes about shit that was going on in the neighborhood. Her brother was one of the dope boys who hung out down the street, but he forbade her to hang out. I knew she used me as a scapegoat, but I didn't mind because I used her too.

"Let's go before Angela comes out," I told her so we could move from in front my home.

If she saw me out talking to Ray, she would have a fit. The last time I tried to introduce the two, she went ballistic. I didn't know why, but it was something about the way she looked at Ray and yelled, *"Bitch, you ain't got no friends!"* to me that made me eerie. But fuck that. I didn't have anybody else.

"I just don't understand why you can't have friends, Reign. That shit is just some weird shit."

"You just said it; the bitch weird. Last night, she slapped me because I went into Mr. Gary's house to eat. I was hungryyy," I whined so she could get my point.

"I don't like how she talks to you. She calls you all out yo' name all in front of people like that shit cool. Especially when she calls you fat."

"Well, I am fat."

"So fucking what? You're pretty."

"You really think I'm pretty?"

"Yes, you are, and you not as big as people try to make it seem. You just got a whole lot of ass," she said and pinched me on the butt. She wasn't lying. I was big but most of my weight was in my ass and thighs. "You have long ass hair and the cutest dimples. You need to just start doing better for yourself and stop letting people bring your self-esteem down. What are you gonna do in a year when you're eighteen? You say you wanna leave her house, but I don't ever hear you mention college. So you gotta figure this shit out. See, my life all figured out. I'mma just say fuck my brother, meet me a dope boy, and live the rest of my life by my pool, spending all my nigga's money."

We both burst out into a fit of laughter. I swear she always said this, and I was starting to think she wasn't lying.

"Honestly, I think you should sing. I mean, you have the voice."

"Girl, I'm not that good." I stopped walking to look at her. I loved singing, but I didn't think I had what it took to do it.

"That's your problem. Stop doubting yourself so much. Bitch, you sing like Beyoncé and Mariah Carey. They ain't got shit on you, Reign."

"I don't know about Mariah, bitch." I playfully nudged her arm.

Just hearing her boasting about my singing made me feel good inside, but I still didn't think I was that good enough to sing in front of thousands of people.

Ever since I was a kid, I've always sang. Even until this day; I used it as my therapy. Because I couldn't go outside much, I would sit in my bedroom window for hours just singing my heart away. The only person, other than Ray, who ever told me I could sing, was Mr. Gary. Many times, I would imagine myself on stage opening up for thousands of people, but that was wishful thinking. I also knew how to play a guitar, but because my mother was so cruel, she broke it into many pieces.

One night, she called my name to rub her back, and when I didn't respond, she came bursting into my room. I was sitting in my window singing and playing my guitar, and before I knew it, it was ripped from my hands. The first swing was to my head, but I guess she wasn't satisfied. She smashed it into the wall nonstop, and before I knew it, it had shattered into a million pieces. Just thinking about that day still hurt me to my soul. My guitar was the only thing I had to my name that I enjoyed. I swear one day, I was gonna get far away from that lady and never look back.

3

Reign

The sound of my door creaking made me look over. I knew it wasn't my mother because normally, she'd bust in. When I looked over, Greg was creeping in like a thief in the night. I quickly pulled my cover over my legs because I was wearing a small pair of shorts.

"Greg, get the fuck out my room before I scream for my mother."

"She won't hear you because she gone. Now let me get some of this fat pussy. I'll throw you a couple bucks," he said with a few dollar bills balled inside of his hand.

"I don't want your money! Get the fuck out!"

"Nah, baby girl. You gon' let me smell this." He pulled my cover off me. The look in his eyes was creepy, making me scared.

"Please leave." I began to cry.

He pulled his pajama pants down, exposing his drawl-less body. His dick stood at attention, creeping me out more. I began to kick at him, but it didn't faze him one bit.

Wham!

He slapped the shit out of me and climbed on top of me. I couldn't do shit but cry because I could see he was serious.

"Pleeeease! Noooo!" I sobbed as he tried to enter me.

"Open these big ass legs, bitch." he said, prying my legs open further.

The minute he put his dick at my opening, the sound of my mother's voice could be heard.

"What the fuck going on in here!"

I closed my eyes, thanking God.

"It's not what you think, baby! Her fat ass came on to me, talking 'bout she had a few dollars for me!" he lied.

"Mom, he's lying!" I was still crying. I lifted from my bed, still shook up.

"Baby, you know I ain't lying."

"He's lying! He was gonna rape me!"

"Bitch, don't nobody want you! You ain't shit but a fat hoe! Get yo' shit, and get the fuck out my house!"

"But he's lying, Ma! I would never—"

"Get the fuck out, hoe!" she screamed, and I couldn't believe she was serious. She had that look in her eyes that she wore whenever she was gonna beat my ass.

Just seeing her facial expression I knew she wasn't playing. I shook my head and walked over to my closet. I began to fill my backpack with the little bit of shit I had to my name.

"I don't have anywhere to go." I looked back at her, hoping she would realize I didn't have anyone but her.

"You should have thought of that before you tried to fuck my man. You got five minutes," she said and walked out the room, followed by Greg's ole nasty ass.

I continued to pack my back, and when I was done, I went into the restroom. I had another empty bag that I filled with my hair brush, gel, toothpaste and toothbrush. I then walked into the kitchen and tossed inside my bag the few packs of noodles I had bought myself. I walked out the kitchen and headed towards the front door. I shot my mother one last look in hope she would show an ounce of sympathy, but she never bothered to look up. Instead, she put her crack pipe to her lips and used the lighter, that didn't have the metal piece, to light the pipe.

Again, I shook my head and walked out the door. When I got into the hall, I looked at Mr. Gary's door, wondering was he home. I wanted to ask him if I could stay, but I thought against it because my mother always threatened to call the police. Because I was a minor, I would be considered a runaway, and I would for sure be going to a foster home or placement.

I zipped up my windbreaker before stepping off the porch. I looked out into the air, and tears began to pour from my eyes. I had three backpacks to my name with nowhere to go. The only person I could think about was Raylen. I looked towards her home, and it was empty, which was unbelievable. However, that was perfect because I didn't have to worry about being teased.

I headed towards her house, and when I made it to her front door, I knocked twice. I waited for a few moments, and I knew someone was home because I could hear kids running through the house. Suddenly, the door was flung open, and her brother stood there with a bowl in his hand. His eyes were bloodshot red like he smoked a pound of weed. Instead of him greeting me, he stood here like he wondered what the fuck I wanted.

"Is Raylen here?" I asked followed by a sigh.

"In the back," he said, then walked off, leaving me standing at the door.

I shook my head and stepped inside. Miesha, who was Rayvon's baby mother, sat on the couch as her kids ran up and down the hall. I headed down the hall until I reached Ray's door. The smell of Victoria's Secret Mango Melon seeped from underneath the door and that told me she had just showered. Twisting the knob, I peeked inside, and she was sitting on the bed lotioning her legs. Her music was blasting, and she had clothes sprawled out on her bed. When she looked up, she had a huge smile that was quickly whipped away when she noticed my tears.

"What's wrong?" she asked with a worried expression.

"You think I could crash here for a few days?"

"Umm...sure. My mother won't mind. Tonight, I'm going out if you wanna come. If not, you could stay here while I'm gone."

"Nah, I'm cool on going out. Plus, I don't have clothes to go out in," I said, taking a seat on her bed.

She looked over to her closet, then back to me. "Okay," was all she said because she for damn sure didn't have shit I could fit.

"Do you mind if I take a shower?"

"Reign, of course, I don't mind. Make yourself at home. You could crash here as long as you need to. Rayvon moved with his bm, so his room is available. You could crash in there. When my mother comes from work, I'll let her know what's up. And when I get back tonight, you could tell me whatever that bitch did to you."

"Thank you soooo much, Ray. I swear I appreciate you so much." I lifted up to hug her.

"That's what friends are for." She smiled.

"Have fun, and be safe," I told her, then headed into the bathroom.

She was fully dressed, so I knew she would be gone by the time I was done.

By the time I was done, I felt so much better. Although I cried my eyes out, not believing what my mother had done, I felt good to finally be out of that house. I had school tomorrow, but right now, school was the last thing on my mind. I needed to find somewhere to lay my head.

I knew I could crash here, but I didn't want to. I would lie here for a few months, but in the meantime, I was gonna try to figure it out. I had a while until my birthday, and the moment I turned eighteen, I would go live in a shelter if I had to. That way, I could get some housing, then focus on going to college. I only had a few credits left to make up because I pushed myself to finish on time.

"What you doing in my room?" Rayvon said, walking into the room.

"Umm...um...Ray said I could crash in here for a few weeks. My mom kicked me out," I added so he would understand what was going on.

"Yeah, yo' ass just bet not break my bed," he shot over his shoulder as he walked out.

I swear I was tired of everybody making fun of my weight. That was another thing that would go on my bucket list: working out. I really didn't care about losing weight; I just wanted to tone up. I wasn't doing this for nobody; I was doing it for myself. I hated always being tired. When I got out of bed, I had to practically roll. One day, I was gonna get in shape, and like I said, it wasn't to please the world. It would be for my health.

Truth

Pulling up to the block, I was furious. This nigga's, Mel, bread was short, and the nigga thought shit was cool. Every time he turned his money in, he was short a hunnit or two. By the time I finished counting it, he would be long gone. He knew what the fuck he was doing because he would never answer his phone. A nigga was so busy with daily life shit I would forget about it, however, I wrote that shit down every time. This nigga was at six bands, and although it wouldn't hurt my pockets, it was the point.

I pulled up to the block, and as usual, niggas were outside shooting dice. I spotted Mel amongst the crowd, so I parked my whip and jumped out. When I walked up on him, my first intention was to pull him to the side, but because the nigga had a handful of money, that shit made my blood boil.

"Yeah, nigga, keep shooting because I need my six bands," I told him and posted up on the wall.

When the nigga turned around, he looked at me like I had shit on me.

Wham!

I reached back and slapped the shit out of him. If he wanted to square up, I ain't have no problem with it. But this slap I just gave his ass was to let him know he was a bitch. I stood back and waited for the nigga to say some slick shit. Everyone that stood around just watched in awe. The entire dice game froze. Niggas knew when it came to my bread I didn't play. I put a sack in all these niggas' hands, and everyone was treated equal. I was the king of my streets, but I fucked with everybody the same.

I didn't look down on niggas who were broke. Actually, I encouraged niggas to get on my level. Even if they didn't want to hustle, I'd helped put niggas in school or start a businesses. I was what you called a community nigga. I made sure everyone in my community was straight. On a regular basis, I helped the needy, but I wasn't gonna help you if you didn't want to help yo' self.

"Here's the muthafucking list," I spat and threw the paper at him. "That shit got every day you dropped the bag off to me and exactly how much the shit was. Nigga, every time you do a drop, yo' shit short. I don't know how you gon' get my six g's, but I ain't putting no more work in your hand until you do. And if you wanna go work for the next nigga, you free to go. However, you won't be selling shit 'round here."

Mel didn't say shit. He tried hard to ignore my mug by staring at the paper in his hand.

I walked off and headed into my nigga's, Rayvon, crib. When I walked in, Miesha was on the couch, and her bad ass kids were tearing up these people's house like always. Ignoring her, I headed down the hall and went into his little sister's room. When I knocked on the door, I heard a voice telling me to come in, but it wasn't Raylen's. I pushed the door open, and shorty from down the street was lying in Ray's bed. This was some unusual shit because ol' girl never came down here, and whenever she did, she would only go to the store.

She looked up at me with a shocked expression, and I could tell she was embarrassed. She always wore the same look when she walked by. I never understood why she was always so scared to look at me. I knew it had a lot to do with low self-esteem, and I didn't understand why. True, she was a bit on the plus side, but she had a pretty ass face with hair that reached the middle of her back. She had the prettiest white teeth and a set of dimples that made her smile complete.

"Where Ray at?"

She looked up at me, not believing I had said a word to her. I wanted to laugh, but I didn't want her to be more nervous than she already was.

"She um...ummm...she went out."

I looked down at my watch and saw that it was nearly one in the morning, so I knew she'd be back soon. I had given Ray a pound of weed to stash for me because that nigga, Rayvon, would have smoked my shit up. See, I only let Rayvon sell my dope. He tried to sell weed plenty of times, but he had a bad weed habit. Rayvon was my nigga, and I didn't need an episode like the one with Mel to occur, so I would just tell the nigga no.

"Call her for me."

"I...I don't have a phone."

"A'ight, well, tell her holla at me when she gets back."

"Okay," she replied, so I closed the door.

I wonder what the fuck she doing here? I thought as I made my way back outside.

The minute my feet hit the pavement, my phone began to ring. I knew it was only Tasha, so I answered.

"Yeah?"

"Where you at?"

"I'm in the hood, Tasha."

"A'ight, well, we just leaving the club. Are you hungry?"

"What you had in mind?"

"Well, Sherice and I were gonna go to IHOP."

I knew what that meant. She thought she was slick. Her ass really ain't want to bring a nigga shit; she was just trying to let me know she was going to eat so her ass could stay out all night, and I wouldn't trip.

"Nah, I'm good. You go ahead."

"Okay," she replied and hung up quickly.

I shook my head because I knew her ass like a book.

Katasha and I had been rocking for two years now. No matter how much I told her I didn't want a bitch, she wouldn't take no for an answer. She came on the block all the time just to be under a nigga, and she even started doing shit like holding my work. I guess she was trying to show me she was a rida, and I ain't gone lie. That shit worked. Tasha had heart like a muthafucka. Not only that, but she could pull any nigga she wanted. She was bad, hands down, but sometimes, that shit went to her head.

She didn't carry herself like a bad bitch with class. Instead, she carried herself like a bad thot. All she wanted to do was club and stay out late with her hoe ass friends. She made a good girlfriend, but that was all she was. I wouldn't dare wife her ass because she had a lot of growing up to do. The day I got married, it would be with a bitch who had class, self-respect, and charm.

You heard right, charm. I was a complete asshole, and I needed a chick to balance me out. Now don't get me wrong. I didn't want a pushover-type-chick; I just wanted her to hold me down in a sexy, charming kinda way. With all the daily shit I dealt with, I ain't need a weak bitch, but I needed her grounded.

"Nigga, where the fuck you been?" I asked Rayvon, who came walking up the street.

"Down the street at Porsha's house."

"Nigga, you crazy as fuck." I laughed and shook my head.

His bm was sitting in the living room, with his kids, while he was down the street fucking a thot. Porsha was the hoodest thot of them all. Homies stayed taking turns on her young ass, and this nigga was the only one who worked with feelings.

"Her head, man. Shit fire." He shook his head like the bitch was contagious, and he couldn't stay away.

"Miesha gonna kill that bitch."

"Fuck her."

"You wild. Aye, what's up with ol' girl in yo' crib?"

"Who? Fat Bitch from down the street?"

"Yeah." I nodded. I hated how everyone referred to her as *Fat Bitch*.

"Shit, I guess she staying here for a minute. Her moms kicked her out."

"Damn, that's fucked up."

"Ain't my problem. Bitch just bet not break my fucking bed," he replied and walked off into the house.

Moments later, he came back out, carrying a diaper bag on his shoulder and little Rayvon in his arms. Miesha was right behind him holding their twins' hands.

"A nigga catch you tomorrow," he shot and began packing up his little family.

I stood back and watched them as they drove off like a happy little fam. That shit made me wish I'd hit my goal so I could leave the game. Every man wanted a family; it was just about choosing the right bitch. These days, hoes only wanted two things: dick and a bag. And with me, they were only getting option number one. Now don't get me wrong. I didn't believe in sticking my dick in just anything. Therefore, I only had about two side chicks and my main. They all new about each other, and even Tasha knew about them because she had caught a nigga too many times.

Like any other nigga, I promised I'd stop fucking with them, but it was hard because of our history. Tracy, I had been fucking with for three years, even before Tasha, and Mekol, I had been fucking since high school. Mekol was the girl I was actually supposed to marry, but because of my lifestyle, she wasn't fucking with a nigga.

My entire family liked Mekol and wished I had wifed her a long time ago. Now Tasha, on the other hand, my pops didn't play much into it, but my moms couldn't stand her. Tasha couldn't stand the ground Mekol walked on because at every family function, she was always around. That broad would be at my crib even when I wasn't there. Like I said, my family rocked with her heavy.

The sound of a car door slamming knocked me out my thoughts and made me look over. Raylen had just hopped out some nigga's car, and the way she was tugging at her short ass dress told me she was drunk. The minute she looked over and spotted me, she quickly leaned into the car. I guess she told the nigga to leave because he quickly started the engine and pulled off.

"Who the fuck is that?" I seethed the minute she walked towards me.

"Nigga, why you always clocking me like I'm yo' bitch?" she slurred, trying hard to keep her dress down.

"Because you know I don't play that shit in my hood, yo. Have you forgot we got enemies, and we hustle right here? We don't need the heat right here, ma."

"And did you forget that this was my fucking house and I don't gotta sneak around you niggas?"

"Get fucked up, Ray." I shot her a look to let her know I wasn't playing.

She walked up on me and stood so close I could smell the liquor seeping from her pores. "You wanna fuck me, huh?"

"Girl, get yo' young ass out my face."

"I'll do that, but, nigga, in a month, you won't be saying that shit." She strolled her little ass up the sidewalk and into her house.

What she meant by that smart ass remark was, in four weeks, she was gonna be eighteen years old. I didn't know why, but let her tell it, I was gonna be her first. I couldn't front if I wanted to. She was sexy as fuck, but she was my nigga's little sister.

Heading to my whip, I pulled out my phone to call Tracy. Since Tasha was out doing her, I was gonna go lay up until about five in the morning, then head to my crib. Tomorrow was gonna be a long ass day because I had to reup and roll through all my traps. This was the part of husting I hated, but soon, it would be all over. I just needed to think of a master plan, and I was gonna back up from the game.

5

Reign

"So what you gonna wear tonight?"

"I don't have anything. I'mma just stay locked up in the room."

"Hell no, Reign. It's my birthday party. Let's go down to the mall. I'mma buy you an outfit and hook yo' hair up."

"I can't have you do that. It's your birthday."

"Girl, just get up. I need an outfit anyway."

"Okay," I replied, not feeling like moving. I lifted up from Ray's bed and made my way to the shower.

"I'mma go shower in the front bathroom. Hurry yo' slow ass up," Ray shot, then walked out the room with her towel and shower cap in hand.

The minute I stepped into the shower, the hot water woke me up. I knew after this I would be relaxed, but a bitch would be ready to pass back out. Since the day I got here, I pretty much slept and wrote music. Ray's mom didn't mind me staying, but it was awkward as hell every time I stepped foot into the living room because Rayvon's baby mama always gave me dirty looks. Not to mention, the rush I got whenever Truth came inside.

It was like he found a reason to come into the house every

day, and he would always give me this look I couldn't read. I peeped that Ray was stashing something here for him, but it wasn't my business, so I would always turn to look away. The way they snuck around also told me Rayvon didn't know, and like I said, it wasn't my business.

I pulled the Dove soap from the holder and began lathering my towel. I scrubbed my body and decided to wash my hair, since Ray was gonna flat iron it for me.

Boom!

The sound of the door opening made me quickly cover my body parts. I looked over, and Rayvon stood there. Instead of him walking back out the door, he stood there and watched me. This nigga looked over every last curve on my body like I was a mouth-watering pork chop, making me feel uneasy.

"Can you get out!"

"Don't nobody wanna see yo' fat ass!" he shot and walked out, slamming the door behind him.

I let out a deep sigh, embarrassed, and I knew after this, I would really be scared to go around him.

After soaping up, I hopped out. When I walked into the room, Raylen was sliding on her jeans. She then took off her scarf and let her fresh wrap fall. I watched her closely as she grabbed the weave brush and began brushing it. Although her hair was bomb, I was more caught up in her beauty. My best friend was bomb, and she knew it. Her little curvaceous frame only added to her pretty face.

I began to think about losing some weight; she was body goals. She always got attention, and I wondered if I'd get the same attention if I dropped a few pounds. It had really been on my mind, especially since I had to hear my mother refer to me as fat. I was getting tired of it. I was tired of Tasha and Rayvon's bullshit too. I knew that's why Truth looked at me the way he did. Therefore, it was either lose weight, or run the fuck away from the world.

By the time Ray and I got back from the mall, it was knocking on seven o'clock. The party started nine o'clock, so we were running a little behind. We needed to re-shower, then mess with my hair. On our way back from the mall, we had stopped by the corner bodega and stole my purple cellophane. Ray tried to get me to get red, but I objected. I've been rocking my purple for some time now, and this was my signature color. At school, everyone made fun of me and called me Barney, but I didn't care. Shit, I liked the color and couldn't nobody tell me shit.

When I got out of the shower, I walked into the room, still wrapped in my towel. I stopped in my tracks because Truth was standing in the doorway talking to Ray, who was sitting on the bed. Just the mere sight of him made my love box wet. This man was so damn fine, and he knew it. He was cocky as hell with a mug that would intimidate anyone. He was dressed in a pair of Levi's with a Levi's coat to match; the old school one with the cotton collar. Underneath, he wore a white-tee, and his three chains laid neatly against his crisp shirt. On his head, he wore a gold NY fitted cap and a pair of gold Timbs to match.

"My bad," his sexy, deep voice spoke out.

He walked out the room, and the minute he was out of ears reach, I let out a deep sigh that was suffocating me.

"Bitch, you're so in love with him," Ray said, smiling from ear to ear.

"No, I'm not." I blushed.

Although I lied, I couldn't contain the blushing. I knew she saw right through my lie because she hit me with a smirk and shook her head.

"Well, guess what? Tonight is your chance. You gon' be looking bomb." She stood up and walked over to me. "Now let's do this hair." She tugged at my ponytail holder.

"That man ain't checkin' for me, Raylen. What would a nigga like Truth do with me? I ain't got shit, and I ain't the prettiest in the world."

"That's crazy how much you put yourself down," she spat annoyed. "You will never know how much a man is interested in you until you give it a shot."

"Ray," I spoke and turned in my seat so she could hear me and hear me clearly. "Truth is the hottest nigga in New York. He has plenty money, dresses nice, and let's not forget he has the baddest bitch in the streets."

"That hoe," she replied, rolling her eyes. "Yeah, that's until he finds out she fucking Dax from Jersey and a bunch of other niggas."

I didn't know who the hell Dax was, but what I did know was, that bitch was crazy if it were true. Truth was that nigga, and any bitch would be dumb to cheat on the nigga.

"Well, that's her business. Like I said, he ain't checkin' for me." I turned around to let her know let's continue.

By the time we were done, it was close to nine o'clock, and I felt like a new person. I watched myself in the mirror, and a lone tear slid down my face. I was wearing some tights because I hated how jeans looked on my huge frame. I wore a purple cotton sweater that hung long to cover my ass. The shoulders were cut open, so I felt a slight-bit sexy. My hair was bone-straight with a side part, but what had me so emotional was, I was seventeen, and this was the first time I ever had my hair done. Shit didn't make any sense. Ray had done a great job on it, and I was gonna do everything in my power to keep it straightened.

Satisfied with my look, I headed out the room. I had to stop when I reached the hallway because I could hear loud commotion like there were a hundred people in attendance already. The smell of weed came flowing down the hall, and the DJ had just turned on the music. I was nervous as hell, so I walked out slowly. When I made it to the living room, it was just as I thought, packed. I scanned the room for Raylen, and when I didn't see her, I headed outside. I ran down the few flights of the stoop stairs, and when I spotted her, she was talking to some guy leaning on a red Jaguar. Shifting my attention from her, my eyes landed in the direction of Truth. However, it wasn't Truth who held my gaze. It was like she could smell my presence because she looked over at me and instantly, her face frowned.

"What yo' fat ass looking at, hoe?" my mother shot just as Truth was dropping, what I assumed were drugs, into her hand.

Her sarcasm made him look over, and the frown on his face was as if he were confused on why the hell this lady had spoken to me like that. Not giving her nor Truth none of my energy, I ignored Angela and headed over to Ray.

"Don't let that hoe get to you. We're gonna enjoy our night," she said, then pulled me towards the house.

As she pulled me away, I looked back, and Truth was looking in our direction. I could see he was surprised to see how I was dressed, but he could have been checking Ray out. No lie, she was looking fly as fuck. She wore a little bit to nothing, exposing her thick, slim thighs and her nice, round breasts. I hoped she meant what she said because I was ready to have some fun. I'd never drank in my life, but tonight, everything would change.

Truth

"Bet five or nine."

"Bet," Rayvon said and pulled out his bread.

I rolled the dice with confidence, and of course, I hit a Nina. I scooped up my money and rolled again. I had been on the dice for over two hours because I didn't have shit else to do. The only time I stopped was when a fiend came and called me outside. Since this nigga Mel had fucked up, I had to literally sit on the block and get it on my own. I had other workers, but they ran their own traps. Until I found someone to take Mel's place, I had to get it out of the mud myself. A part of me didn't mind because my profit was doubled.

"So you niggas gonna just shoot dice all fucking night!"

I looked up, and Raylen was standing over the dice game. Before I knew it, she started twerking her ass in front of me. I couldn't do shit but laugh because I could feel Rayvon's eyes grilling us.

"Get fucked up, Ray!" he shot, ready to beat her ass. Nigga knew not to look my way, so he didn't bother.

"Watch out, Raylen, before I gotta fuck yo' brother up," I

told her, but in a whisper, so he could think it was more than what it was.

I did it just to fuck with him because he always talked shit when she was in my face. Every day, when Ray walked past us hanging out, she made it her business to flirt with a nigga. Rayvon always brushed it off as if she were bullshitting, but real shit, she wanted a nigga knee deep in her little pussy. A few times I had gotten tempted, but I'd always brush her off because she was too young. However, she was now officially legal, and she was trying harder than before.

Rayvon's facial expression went sour just that fast and that shit made me laugh more. When I looked over, Ray's sidekick was laughing, but the minute we made eye contact, she dropped her head. I didn't know what was up with this chick, but she was a complete weirdo. She was always so quiet and barely replied when spoken too. She never talked to anyone. Hell, I was surprised she was dressed and out here partying.

"Fuck you laughing at?" I asked her with a frown to make her think I was serious.

"Yo' ass," she sassed, rolling her neck. I couldn't believe she actually spoke.

"Oh, you got a voice now?"

She frowned and nodded her head. Since she wanted to be bold, I left the dice game and walked over to baby girl and stood right in her face, invading her personal space.

She looked up at me nervously.

"What's up, Truth?"

I looked up and was met with Porsha. She continued to walk past me, and I knew now shit was about to get ugly. Taking my focus off baby girl, I watched as she walked over to Rayvon. She walked up in his face, so I looked over to where his baby mama was. I could see the bullshit coming because she wore a frown as she lifted from the sofa. She walked right over to Rayvon, and when she was in arm's reach, her neck began popping and rolling. Porsha's messy ass hit her with a smirk, and everybody knew what that meant; they were fucking.

Instead of walking over to them, I headed outside to catch some sells. I wanted no parts of their dick and pussy drama. As soon as I stepped outside, smoker, Angela, was standing by the curb. I thought back to when her and ol' girl mugged each other and wondered what that was all about. Angela was a straight fiend from around the way, and I ain't never known her to have any family, other than her smoked-out nigga, Greg.

"Damn, you back already?" I shook my head because only a couple hours had gone by since she came and copped.

"I didn't know y'all was having a party," she said and looked around me towards the door.

"Man, what you need?"

"I was wondering if I could get a few beers."

"Yep, five dollars each can."

"Five dollars? Nigga they only one-fifty at the store!"

"Well, take yo' begging ass to the store. Bye, Felicia." I walked off, and I could hear her smacking her lips.

"What's up, Truth? Why you ain't in the party?"

I turned around to Raylen. She looked tipsy as hell and was wiping sweat from her face, which told me she had been shaking her ass.

"Shit, just tryna get some bread."

"That's all you do." She playfully rolled her eyes.

"What's wrong with that shit?"

"A lot. Nigga, you rich as fuck. I don't even understand why you out here trappin' anyway. Shit risky."

"Man, mind yo' business."

"You is my business." She smirked.

Before I could reply, Rayvon came out of the crib, followed by his bm, and of course, they were in a full-fledged argument.

"Nigga, you got me fucked up! I ain't dumb! You and that nasty hoe fucking! I swear you nasty as fuck! Every nigga in the hood dun' fucked that bitch!"

"Man, ain't nobody fucking that girl. She was just saying what's up."

"Nah, that was more than a, 'what's up'! Fuck you, nigga!

I'm out this bitch!" she shouted in his face.

She knew what she was doing. No matter what this nigga Rayvon did, he was in love with his girl. The nigga stayed chasing behind her like a puppy ass nigga, so more than likely, he was about to roll with her.

"That nigga a pussy for that hoe," Raylen said, watching her brother hop into the passenger seat of the Lexus he had copped Miesha.

I couldn't do shit but chuckle because Ray was right. Nigga was a straight simp.

Raylen walked back into the house, and I stood on the curb for a few. I looked down at my watch, and when I noticed it was almost one a.m., I knew this party would soon be over. A few people had already shook, but it was still a few people left. *Damn, this bitch been too quiet,* I thought about Tasha. Her ass was supposed to come to the party, but she ain't never show up. Something was starting to get to me with her. She was up to something, but I couldn't put my finger on it. I wasn't the type to chase a bitch down, so instead of calling her, I headed back into the house.

Come 2:41 in the morning, the party had finally come to an end. Because a nigga didn't wanna go home, I stayed behind chilling with my nigga, Band, and fucked with Raylen. Her little sidekick had just gone into the room about twenty minutes ago, and Band was about to roll.

Saying fuck it, I decided to crash here for the night because I was too faded, and I lived kinda far. Fucking with Raylen, her ass kept pouring a nigga cup after cup.

I headed into Raylen's room and kicked off my shoes. I wasn't gonna take my clothes off because I was gonna have to be up before Rayvon came. If that nigga saw me in his sister's bed, he would die. Little did he know, I spent many nights in her bed. Anytime I was too tired to go home, because I had hugged the block all night, I'd walk in and tell her to scoot over.

"Yo' ass not sleeping with me, Truth. You sleep too fucking wild," she said, mugging me as I lay in her bed comfortably.

"Man, lie yo' ass down," I told her, patting the side of me.

"Yeah, I'mma lie down a'ight," she replied and merged into the restroom.

I tried hard to close my eyes, but each time, a nigga's head began spinning. I began tossing and turning so I could shake this feeling but wasn't shit working. When I heard the door open to the restroom, I didn't bother looking up. I knew it was Ray because the scent of her Beyoncé perfume.

When she finally climbed in the bed, her body slid next to mine. I went to throw my arm over her like I normally did, and I got the shock of my life. My eyes shot open, and I knew I wasn't tripping. I turned to look at her, and she stared at me like an exotic cat. My eyes roamed her naked body. I looked back up at her, and it was like her eyes were calling for a nigga.

Caught up, I didn't know what to do. I felt my dick rising in my jeans, and my shit was starting to feel like it was gonna explode. Before I knew it, she had lifted up and was pulling my pants down. My mind was saying stop her, but a nigga's dick was saying, *"Hurry the fuck up."*

I lay in the bed with my dick standing towards the ceiling. Raylen had begun stroking my shit and was now getting ready to climb on top. This was my chance to back out, but the sexy gestures she was making had a nigga ready to tear her little ass up. She was squatting over me, standing on her feet. She grabbed my dick and positioned it at her opening. Her pussy was dripping wet, making it easy for her to slide down on my dick.

"Ohhh, shit, Truth." She instantly began moaning and shit.

"Man, be quiet," I told her, hoping no one heard her.

Her mom was in her room, which was all the way down the hall, but for some odd reason, I didn't want her homegirl to hear us.

"My mom can't hear us, and Reign prolly sleep."

Reign, I thought as Ray began to ride me. I put my hands behind my head because this was how I was gonna bust my nut. I was too faded for too much bouncing and shit.

As Raylen bounced on my dick, I watched her closely. I didn't know if I was just drunk or what ,but a nigga had drifted off into a daze. I began to think of days after this day how she would act on the block. I hoped she understood she needed to keep this shit between us, and not because of her brother, but because of my girl. I knew Tasha hearing some shit like this would kill her. I had already put her through enough, but with this, she'd prolly kill a nigga. I knew I had some fire ass dick, which was why I chose not to put it on Ray. I didn't need her ass tripping out on me and exposing what we had done.

"It's not good to you?" she asked, bringing me from my thoughts.

I looked up at her. She had stopped riding me and had this confused look on her face.

"You straight, ma. Stop bugging, yo."

"Nigga, you straight blanked out on me," she said and began moving slowly.

I wanted to holla at her, but I didn't want to come off fucked up, so I chose my words wisely. "Man, you know we can't tell nobody about this shit, Ray."

"Oh, so that's what's wrong?" Again, she stopped. "Who I'mma tell, Truth? My brother would kill me, and don't worry, nigga, yo' dick ain't that good," she said seriously, but I knew that was a lie.

I let out a slight chuckle and grabbed at her waist. Now that we got that understood, I was gonna beat her little pussy up and take my ass to sleep.

Reign

"What the hell?" My eyes shot open because I could feel someone tugging at my pajama pants.

I felt it in my sleep, and I began having a horrible dream about Greg. It was like I was reliving the day my mom kicked me out, but when I opened my eyes, it wasn't Greg.

"I'm about to get some of this fat pussy, and yo' ass bet not say shit."

"Get out before I scream for your mom."

"You ain't gone do shit 'cause I'mma beat yo' ass. You 'bout to give me some pussy, and I swear if you tell anybody about this, I'mma murk yo' ass. You ain't gon' have me on the block looking stupid for fucking with yo' big ass," Rayvon shot seriously.

What I didn't understand was, if I was so fat, why the fuck was he violating me? The look in his eyes when he said he would murk me looked like they held some truth. I knew he was serious just like I knew he was serious about taking my prized possession because he had basically ripped my pants off.

Rayvon was fine as hell, just like Truth, but right now, he was the ugliest person on Earth to me. Any girl in the world would have probably died for this moment due to his street statute alone. However, right now, he looked desperate, like I was the last piece of pussy on Earth.

"Spread yo' shit," he demanded but basically spread them himself. He wasted no time putting his dick at my opening, and I began to pray that someone would walk through the door.

The minute he got the head in, I was already crying. It felt like he was ripping my insides apart, but no matter how much I cried, it fell on deaf ears.

"Oh, this some fat, virgin pussy." He hissed as he shoved his dick in harder.

It took everything in me not to scream. There was always a house full of people, so I didn't understand why anyone hadn't come in.

I lay still with tears rolling down my cheeks, and Rayvon continued to assault the only precious jewel I had. This wasn't how I imagined my first sexual encounter would be. I always imagined that Truth would be the one between my legs and making love to me while I sang. I fell into a complete daze as Rayvon growled and pumped in and out of me. It was like my whole body went numb, and even the tears stopped falling. I was so deep in my thoughts, I never even realized he had bust his nut and was walking out the door. What brought me back to was the sound of his voice.

"You heard what I said, fat bitch. You tell somebody about this, I'mma kill yo' ass." And with that, he walked out the room.

I wanted to go hop in the shower because I felt disgusted, but my body wouldn't let me move. Instead, I turned to my side, and on came the tears again. Not only did he violate me, but he also threatened me. I couldn't do shit but cry, and before I knew it, I had dozed off with a broken heart.

Three months later

Every day, I lay around embarrassed, not wanting to face Rayvon. I stayed locked up in his old room, praying Raylen wouldn't ask me to go outdoors. It was like God was working in my favor because lately, she had become slightly distant. She was always hanging outside with Truth and Rayvon and the rest of their homies who hung out. From time to time, she would come in to chill with me, but she never asked me to come outside. What she did do was constantly bring me food.

After the incident with Rayvon, it was like I fell into a deep depression, and all I did was eat. From me just sitting on my ass and eating all day, I knew I was getting bigger, and that was another reason I didn't want to go outside. However, today, I needed some air. I felt like I was suffocating being cooped up in this room.

I slid into my purple and black retro Jordans that Ray had brought me and grabbed my purple jacket that was also complementary of Raylen. I didn't know what this girl was doing, but lately, she has been having a lot of money. She always bought us food to eat, clothing, and she had mentioned she was gonna buy a car soon.

When I stepped outside, there was a load of niggas lingering around. The first person I spotted was Truth, and when he looked at me, I quickly looked away. Shortly after, my eyes connected with Rayvon. He instantly frowned his face like I was the most disgusting thing on Earth. I put some pep in my step and hurried up the street towards the store. I had forty dollars I had gotten from Ray, so I was gonna buy me a pickle and some tropical punch Kool-Aid.

As I walked down the street, I noticed a few flyers plastered on the walls and boards of the abandoned buildings. The words *Open Mic* caught my attention, so I snatched the form down and began reading as I walked. It was a modern nightclub called Bleu Cabana that hosted open mic every Wednesday. Reading over the contact information, Tony was the man to see. I shoved the paper into my pocket. I actually contemplated calling the number. The Bleu Cabana was more of a soulful club with a much older crowd, so if I did consider going, I wouldn't run into the neighborhood knuckle heads.

On my way back from the store, I continued past the house and headed to see Mr. Gary. I was praying like hell I didn't run into my mother, so I knocked with ease. When he opened the door, a smile spread across his face as if he were happy to see me.

"Come on in here, child," he said and opened the door further.

I walked in, and like always, the smell of soul food lingered in the air. I wasn't even hungry, but in an instant, my stomach began to growl.

"It smells good up in here. What you hooked up?"

"Help yourself, child. It's oxtails, peas, and white rice."

I smiled at just the sound of oxtails. I went over to wash my hands and began to make me a plate.

"I'm glad you got away from that evil winch next door, but where you staying?" He looked at me from the rim of his glasses.

"I've been staying up the street with Raylen."

"Raylen?" he asked puzzled. I didn't reply, so he continued. "You be careful down there. All them drugs and stuff those youngsters selling now, I don't want you getting caught up in that mess. And you make sure you stay the hell away from that damn Truth. That boy out here passing out that poison."

"Gotcha," was all I could reply with.

I knew he was only looking out for me, but Truth didn't seem like much harm. He was actually cooler than I thought. The night of Ray's party was the longest I'd ever been in his presence, and he seemed pretty laid back.

"You know Tony holding open mic down there at the Cabana. You should gone up there, Reign."

"I just saw the flyer. I'm thinking 'bout it."

"I'll come support, baby girl." He smiled and walked back over to take a seat.

I was happy he walked off because I was ready to scarf my food down.

Once I was done eating, I stayed around to talk with Mr. Gary for a couple hours. I really didn't feel like going back down the street, but it was time I went home. I told Mr. Gary I would see him soon and headed out the door. I took my time walking up the street because a crowd was formed in front of our building. As I got closer, Tasha was in Truth's face talking mess.

I didn't know what they were arguing about, but she did say, "Why that bitch always in your face?"

I wondered who she could be talking 'bout, but I would never figure it out because every girl in the hood stayed in his face. Everybody wanted a piece of Mr. Truth, and Tasha knew it.

"Bitch, what yo' fat ass looking at?" Tasha shot, looking at me.

I swear I'm tired of this bitch, I thought, mugging her back. "You, hoe," I replied, not believing I had said it.

I guess Truth couldn't believe it either because he looked at me with a shocked expression.

"Oh, I got your hoe," she said like she was gonna charge at me.

Truth grabbed her arm and roughly hemmed her up on the wall. I snickered at her silly ass and headed into the house.

I wasn't 'bout to entertain this cunt bitch any longer because I ain't wanna be starting shit at Ray's crib. Right now, I had to stay here, so I had to be respectful, however, that didn't mean Ray wouldn't whoop her ass. I knew she could only be talking 'bout her. It was evident by the way Tasha looked at Ray. She assumed Ray wanted Truth, but little did she know, I was the one head over heels for him.

I went into Raylen's room, and when I walked in, she wasn't inside. The light was on in the restroom, so I assumed she was using the restroom. However, the sound of weeping caught my attention and made me head over to the door. I knocked lightly, and when I didn't get a response, I slowly opened it.

"Oh my God! Girl, you good?" I ran over to Ray's side to help her up from the floor.

"I can't stop throwing up. It hurts," she said, clutching her stomach.

"Let me get you some water." I walked out and headed into the kitchen.

"Oh, child, you picking up some weight," Mrs. Arnold said, looking over my body.

The sound of Rayvon chuckling, along with Miesha, made me look up. They were both laughing like shit was funny. Instead of replying, I reached into the fridge and grabbed a bottled water. I quickly walked back into the restroom and handed it to Ray.

"Thanks." She wiped her mouth and struggled to open it.

"Ray, you good?" I looked at her from the side of my eyes. She knew the look I was giving her, and she shook her head *no* out of embarrassment.

"Ray, a nigga 'bout to head..."

We both looked up as Truth walked into the room. When he spotted us, he walked over to the restroom door and looked down at Raylen. Her eyes shot open wide, and Truth frowned.

"Fuck wrong with you?" he asked her through the slits of his eyes.

"Nothing, I'm fine." She wiped her mouth and got up from the floor. She walked past Truth, and he was still grilling her.

I knew then that Truth was thinking the same shit I was thinking; her ass was pregnant. The way he was looking, I knew he wasn't feeling it, and it was only a matter of time before he would tell Rayvon. Truth was like the big brother 'round here. Wherever Rayvon lacked, he was right there to pick up the pieces. He always grilled Ray about the things she did, so I knew her being pregnant would only piss him off.

"Yeah, you look ill as hell. You need to get on top of that. Anyway, I'm out for the day, so put that shit up."

"You out?"

"Yeah. I'mma go fuck with Tasha's ass. She tripping."

"Fuck her, but yeah, a'ight." Ray waved him off and headed for her bed. She plopped down, and Truth made his way out the door.

"I'mma go out for a moment. You need something?" I asked.

"A pregnancy test, I guess." She shook her head and grabbed her purse from the dresser. "Get me a Ginger Ale too, and, Reign, don't let no one see the test."

"Okay, I got you."

I took the money from her hand and headed for the room to grab my purse. When I made it outside, Truth was just getting into his car, and Tasha had just closed her door. Her mumbling something under her breath made him look over to me, and our eyes locked as he held my gaze. Again, she said some shit that made me turn my head. I knew he was only looking at me the way he was because like everyone else, I was fat.

I let out a deep sigh and headed up the street. By the time I got to the store, I was tried as fuck. I headed in and purchased the items for Ray and grabbed myself some Skittles and Flaming Hot Funyuns. When I reached into my purse to tuck Ray's change, the flyer from the Bleu Cabana fell to the ground. I picked it up and read over the details. *Oh, what the hell,* I thought as I headed towards the nightclub. I was just gonna check it out because I was sure I couldn't get past the security, but I was gonna give it a shot. I mean, it would be good for me to get away and let off some steam.

When I made it to the Cabana, there were a few people outside and the security guard. I walked over and stuck my head inside to get a feel for the crowd. The place was pretty packed inside, but the crowd was much older and calm. I looked over at the security, and I recognized him from the neighborhood as Larry.

"Hey, Larry."

"'Sup, child. How's Angela?"

"She's fine. I actually went to go get her some cigarettes," I lied so he wouldn't know her ass actually kicked me out.

"Oh, okay. What brings you 'round this way?"

"Ummm...well, I was hoping I could sing for the open mic tonight."

"Now you know I can't let you in here. They sell liquor; they could lose their license."

"Well, I don't drink, Larry. Please? This will be my way to let off a little steam. I mean, you know, dealing with Angela and all."

He looked at me already knowing. Everyone around the hood knew how it was dealing with that woman. People would always tell her about herself, but she didn't care. Her crack pipe and Greg were her only concerns. Well, that was until she caught Greg cheating. Greg laid up in the dirtiest motels with other crackheads and prostitutes was a norm. My mom would catch him, then always take him back.

"Go on in there. Ask Tony, he's the owner."

"Okay."

I rushed off after thanking him. I headed inside, and my stomach started turning from the thick clouds of smoke. Other than that, the place felt relaxing. The lights were dim, there was a huge backdrop on the stage of a sunset and water, and the woman on stage singing brought calm to the atmosphere. She was blowing the hell out of "Ebony Eyes" by Rick James, and she was doing a great damn job. She had a strong voice like Anita Baker, but she looked mixed like Lena Horne. She was beautiful, and the way people cheered her on when she hit her notes told me she was a regular.

"Hey, chile. What brings you in here?" A lady approached me wearing an apron and carrying drinks on a tray.

"Umm, I'm looking for Tony. I wanted to see if I could audition."

"You look mighty young." She shifted her weight from one hip to another.

"Well, I'm only here to sing. I don't drink, and I just need somewhere to unwind," I replied, and she looked me up and down.

She got silent for a moment, then let out a deep sigh. "I'm gonna give you a chance up there. I can lose my job because of your age. Now I'll make a deal with you. If you're good, you can sing weekly. If you waste my damn time up there, Tony will chew me out and that will be your ass," she sassed, and I smiled. "You up next. And no damn rapping." She laughed and slid her ink pen into her bun. "Go over there and tell the DJ what instrumental to play."

"Okay."

"Jana," she added, telling me her name.

"Reign, Jana. I really appreciate you."

"You're welcome, Reign." She smiled and headed over to a table.

I walked over and told the DJ what song I wanted him to play. At first, he looked at me strangely, then hit me with a thumbs up. I stood off to the side, and my heart was racing. I wasn't really nervous, but I was anxious as hell. I needed to relieve some stress, and this was gonna help me. When it was my time to go up, I walked onto the stage, and I could feel everyone's eyes watching me. I looked into the crowd and became nervous. Jana was watching me like a hawk when the beat dropped. When it was my time to sing, I gave it all I had.

"I'm young and I'm old
I'm rich and I'm poor

I feel like I've been on this earth many times before
Once I was a white Gazelle
On horseback riding free
Searching in the darkness for a piece of me..."

I sang my heart out to Teena Marie's "Deja Vu (Been Here Before)," and judging by the way people started whistling, I had to have done a great job. As I continued to sing, I saw a Caucasian man run over to Jana. I couldn't hear what he was saying, but I could see she was ignoring him. He then focused on me, and his angry face turned sorrowful. I guess it was my facial expression while I sang that captured the heart and souls of not only him, but my audience. Anytime I sang, I sang from my soul. Like I said, this was my therapy, and the aroma of the lyrics soothed me every time.

By the time I was done, everyone stood to their feet. Even Jana was clapping with the tray underneath her arm pits. The Caucasian guy, who I assumed was the owner, stood there appalled. I smiled as I looked around the room at my new family. I tried hard to get familiar with the faces of the people who sat in the front rows and even in the back. I knew after tonight, I was gonna be back weekly as Jana offered. Already I felt at ease with comfort.

Reign

"So are you really considering getting rid of it?"

"I don't know. I can't have a baby. Reign, my mom would kill me. Not only her, but Rayvon would die too."

"Don't forget Truth. He act like he your big brother."

Instead of her replying, she shook her head. I could see it all in her face; she was scared to death. I could also tell she ain't wanna get rid of the baby. However, it may have been the best decision based on she ain't no who the father was. She said it was possible it could be Devin around the corner, but she wasn't sure because the condom broke with Akeem from 7th Street. And this was exactly why I said it may be best she got rid of it.

"Anyway, enough about me. What's up with you, friend? Why you always cooped up in this room? And where have you been? I noticed you disappear every Friday night. Let me find out you going on dates and shit." She smirked, looking over at me.

"No, no dates. And I don't know. I just like to sit in here and think, I guess," I lied.

The real reason was, I was so damn depressed my weight

was picking up tremendously. The only place I would go was to the Cabana to sing. I still hadn't told Ray because I ain't want her to feel like she had to come by to support me. The Cabana had become my escape from reality, and I had even used it to escape Raylen. She was so tied in with Truth and Rayvon, and I tried my best to stay clear of them.

"On Fridays, I just go sit down with Mr. Gary." Again, I lied.

"Oh, okay. Poor Mr. Gary," she cooed and dropped her head.

I didn't know why, but it felt like Ray wasn't telling me something. She looked so out of it at times, and I knew my best friend. However, I didn't pry in people's business.

"Reign, come on in here and eat, baby."

Ray and I looked up to her mother, who opened my room door.

"Ohhh, Raylen, I didn't know you were here. Food's ready."

"Okay, Ma. Thanks."

"Why the long face? What's going on with you girls? You guys always look so gloomy. You're too young with a whole life ahead of you to always look so depressed." Mrs. Arnold shook her head, looking at Ray and me.

"We're okay, Ma."

"No, y'all not. Reign, are you pregnant?" she asked, and my eyes darted over to Ray.

I didn't mean to, but I couldn't help it. Shit, I wasn't the one out here fucking. Well, other than the fact that her son had practically raped me, but it was Ray, not me.

"I know it ain't yo' ass, Raylen Unique Arnold."

Ray dropped her head and that was all the confirmation she needed. She looked at Ray with so much disappointment, but she didn't attack her. I thought about Angela and how this would have gone completely different had it been me. My teeth would be on the floor, and my baby would have been punched right out of me. I looked between the two, and when Ray didn't say anything, Ms. Arnold spoke.

"You're getting rid of it." She fumed and walked out the door.

When it closed ,Ray looked over at me. "I ain't getting rid of this baby. She's not about to make me because she wants me to. It's my decision, Reign. Yes, I live here, but she doesn't take care of me, and I don't ask. I do everything for myself."

"I don't understand why everyone makes having kids a big deal. It's a blessing, best friend, and if you wanna have it, I'll support you."

"Thank you." She faintly smiled, and a tear came tumbling down her face.

The question was, whoever the daddy was, was he gonna be supportive? However, like I said, I was gonna support my best friend and help her understand that having a child wouldn't have to be the worst decision.

"Reign, you sure is picking up some weight, child."

"I know, Mr. Gary. It's like all I do is eat. Since my mom kicked me out, I've been depressed."

"Well, you watch yourself now. You know it's not about what you eat, it's about how much you eat. Just watch those calories. How's that hoe doing anyway?" he asked, making me laugh so hard I spit a little of my grape soda out.

"I don't know. When I see her, she doesn't speak to me. She buys her drugs from Truth and be gone 'bout her business."

"Good. You stay out her way. Now I don't know how long you gon' be down at that fast ass girl's house, but don't waste your life there. You'll be eighteen soon. You get you a job and get far away from here."

"I am, Mr. G. I don't wanna stay here all my life. Ain't nothing here for me."

I dropped my head and thought of all the shit I had to deal with daily. I didn't ask to be here, and at times, I even contemplated suicide. It seemed like the only two people in the world who loved me were Mr. Gary and Ray. The rest of the world came down on me and hard like rain. I spent ninety-five percent of my time living in sorrow. I watched how everyone around me was normal and cheerful. I knew I wasn't supposed to question God, but I found myself asking him all the time, *Why Me?* I just didn't understand. I wasn't a bad child, and I damn sure ain't do wrong by others.

"You need to just figure things out with your music. Speaking of, I picked something up for you." He lifted from his La-Z-Boy chair and headed into the back of his apartment. "Now it ain't much. I got it from the thrift shop down on 36th." He walked into the living room holding a black wooden guitar.

My eyes beamed as Mr. Gary handed me the guitar. "Awww, Mr. G, thank you." I jumped to my feet and hugged him so tight. I was so damn happy I could cry.

"You don't have to thank me, Reign. You deserve it." He smiled with glossy eyes.

Damn, Mr. G was dope. I swear he went above and beyond for me when he didn't have to. Mrs. Gary was the same way when she was alive. She was like the grandma I never had. My mother's mother passed before I was born, so I never got a chance to meet her. My mother had me kinda old, and believe it or not, my entire life, she was on crack. Even thinking back to a child, I couldn't remember a time when she was sober.

"I sang at Bleu Cabana!" I shouted excitedly because I had forgotten to mention it.

Mr. Gary's eyes shot open wide, and he smiled.

"They loved me. I've been back twice since, and each time, it gets better. At first, the owner was tripping off my age, but everyone there begged him to let me stay."

"I'm proud of you. Maybe I'll come on down one night."

"You should do that. You know you may find a wife." I nudged him in the shoulder playfully.

"Nobody wants my old, lonely ass. I'm gonna die an old and lonely man." He looked off into the air.

Hearing him mention dying hurt me. I couldn't imagine life without Mr. G. However, he was old, and I knew his day would come. I just prayed he was here to see my success. I didn't care. In my heart, I knew God had plans for me, which was why I suffered so much now. My day was gonna come, and I was gonna make Mr. G proud of me.

"You got me, Mr. G." I smiled and looked down at my guitar. I headed for the door because I was anxious to go play.

"Do me one favor, Reign. I'm gonna come down to the Cabana, and you better sing me some Anita Baker. Hatty loved her some Anita. That girl used to be stripping around this house like one of those young girls. Titties hanging down here, but that was my baby."

"Mr. G!" I laughed so hard I doubled over.

I swear this man was crazy but so damn cool. He wasn't lying, though. Mrs. G thought she was young, and she sang beautifully. Whenever I came over, we would do duets. My favorite with her was "Fire & Desire." She would let me sing Teena Marie's part while she sang Rick James' part. I swear I missed that lady.

"I got you. Come on down on Friday nights."

"I'll be there. Love you, child."

"Love you too, young dude." I called him by the nickname I gave him.

I headed down the short few steps, and right when I got down, Angela was coming up. She looked at me, and her face frowned.

"What you looking at, bitch?" She stopped, and her entire neck rolled.

I shook my head and kept walking. I could still feel her watching me, and I swear it took everything in me to not flick her ass the bird. I didn't sweat her, though. I kept on down the street so I could bury myself in my bedroom with my new guitar.

Truth

Three Months Later

"What why you looking like that?"

"I just can't believe you kept that baby. Ray, what the fuck you think gon' happen when this shit hits the fan?" I shook my head at Raylen because her stomach was big as fuck. I mean, everyone knew she was pregnant, but no one knew the baby was mine. "You think this shit gon' be cool? Yo' moms gon' be tripping, and yo' brother and I definitely gon' go to war. You know I don't give a fuck, but that's my nigga. Not to mention, that's yo' bro; I ain't tryna body the boy."

"So what you wanna do because it's not too late?"

"Man, get fucked up, Ray. You almost six months; that's a whole fucking baby."

"Well, I'm just saying because what you not 'bout to do is act like I was tryna trap you. I kept this baby because it's a blessing. Keep shit real. You ain't gotta be here for me or my son."

"Should have thought of that before you kept him."

"Yeah, well, you should have thought of that before you

fucked me raw. Nigga, after you fucked me for the first time, yo' ass came back again for this sweet, young pussy. Save that shit, Truth."

She waved me off and walked into the bathroom. I shook my head, not even trying to finish arguing with her no more. Shit was stupid, and her keeping the baby was even dumber. I wasn't ready for no kids, and I damn sure ain't want one by Raylen. Wasn't shit wrong with shorty, but she came with too many discrepancies. Like her brother for one. Rayvon was my top lieutenant, and I knew there was gonna be some bad blood. Mrs. Arnold definitely would die when she found out. That lady watched me grow up, so I was like family. Man, I wasn't even 'bout to justify why I ain't want the baby; shit, I just didn't want it.

Just as I made it outside, Tracy's car was passing up the block. When she saw me, she stopped so hard she almost fucked up her motor. She pulled right over to the curb, and I could see her head moving like she was already cursing my ass out. I wanted to jump into my whip and pull off, but knowing Tracy, she'd prolly chase a nigga. Therefore, I walked to the car and leaned inside.

"What's up with you, stranger?" she asked.

"Shit, 'bout to turn a corner."

"Damn, you always turning corners, but not my way. Why I ain't seen you?"

"Shit, I've been busy."

"Nah, you ain't busy. You just been having yo' nose wide open for what's her name."

"You know her name, and yeah, that's my bitch," I replied, and she smacked her lips.

This was exactly why I ain't been fucking with Tracy because she was always worried 'bout another bitch. If it wasn't Tasha, it was Mekol. The bitch didn't understand her place.

"That bitch for everybody." She waved me off. "Anyway," she went to say, but that last statement took me by surprise.

I knew how bitches hated on other bitches, but some things bitches said had some truth to them.

"All you bitches for everybody," I replied, deciding not to feed into her bullshit. "Check it, though. I'm out. I got—"

"You so fucking disrespectful!"

I looked over, and Raylen was coming down the steps. My eyes fell to her small stomach, but it was obvious she was pregnant. I looked down at Tracy to see if she heard her, and when she didn't say some slick shit, I knew she couldn't have. Tracy knowing I fucked Raylen would be all over the hood by five p.m. This bitch had a big ass mouth, and she would get a kick out of making Tasha look bad.

"I'm out, ma." I patted her whip and walked away.

When she pulled off, I walked up on Raylen, who was standing at the bottom of the short flight of stairs.

"Yo, what's yo' problem?"

"*You*, nigga. Look, I don't give a fuck who you stick yo' dick in because you ain't my nigga. Just keep that shit on the otha' side of the hood." She curled her lips and headed up the street.

I couldn't even be mad because it was a respect thang. The good thing was, Ray wasn't tryna trap me or even be my bitch. Which was crazy because any chick I stuck this dick in fell madly in love with a nigga. I knew us being a secret played a big part, but what happened when the shit hit the fan? Would that give her the green light to act an ass? Just at the thought alone, I shook my head, realizing that one night was the biggest mistake I'd ever made. After the first time, my dumb ass went back like she said. I mean, it wasn't my fault her pussy was so fucking good. It was actually better than Tasha's *and* any bitch I was smashing right now.

"A nigga finished that first pack."

I turned around, and Rayvon was coming down the steps counting money. He handed me the stack and began making small talk. After about twenty mins, Ray was coming back up the street holding a bag. I watched her as she got closer to us, and our eyes met, but I quickly turned my head.

"This stupid bitch." Rayvon watched her as she went up the stairs.

"Leave lil' sis alone."

"Man, fuck that. I swear when I find out who put that baby in her, I'mma kill the nigga."

"I understand you mad, but that ain't no reason to call her out her name. Nigga, that's yo' little sister."

"I don't give a fuck about all that. Fuck her, that nigga, and that baby," he spat, sounding like he meant every word.

I swear I wanted to hit the nigga in the face with my pistol. He was talking greasy, not knowing I was the nigga who put the baby in her. Just hearing him speak ill on me made me wanna tell him just to see if he was gon' have that same energy.

Instead of replying, I ignored the nigga and waited for him to count the rest of my bread. When he finally handed it all to me, I shoved it in my pocket, and it was my cue to leave. Before I walked away, Rayvon and I both looked up, and Reign was coming up the street. The way his nose turned up I knew he was gonna have some slick shit to say about her too. I watched her as I waited for him to talk to shit.

"Now here comes this fat hoe. Shoes leaning to the side and shit." He chuckled like I was supposed to laugh with him.

I continued to watch Reign, and true, she had picked up some weight, but that didn't give him a reason to talk down on her. Other than her weight, Reign was beautiful. Keep it real, she wasn't as big as most people made her seem. If she dropped about twenty pounds, she'd be perfect. Her body was actually stacked. I swear if she dropped those few pounds, she'd kill the game.

"Man, one day, you gon' get hurt." I shook my head at the nigga and hopped into my whip.

The thought of how Reign looked began to weigh heavy on me. I could tell she was embarrassed and that shit wasn't cool. I hated when Tasha did the shit too. They made fun of this girl because of her weight, and the shit just wasn't cool. Looking down on people, whether they're less fortunate or got the world, was the easiest way to block yo' blessing; a nigga was already living foul.

"That's all the fuck you do is sleep. What's up with you?"

"The fuck you mean, 'what's up'? And close that fucking window."

"It's six in the afternoon, Truth."

"Okay, and?"

"And I want some dick."

Hearing her freaky ass say she wanted to fuck made my dick stand up. Because I was already naked, I pulled the covers back, and her eyes lit up when she saw how hard my dick was.

"Come climb on this muthafucka."

She did as told. She wasted no time coming out that little ratchet ass gown. As she climbed on top of my dick, I grabbed both cheeks and forcefully slid her down on me.

"Ohhhh, Daddy." She started moaning, and I wasn't even killing her shit yet.

That shit only made me go harder. I took my right hand and reached behind her as she was riding all ten inches. I took my thumb and put it right in her ass hole. Just by the look in her eyes, I knew this bitch was feeling what just transpired, so now I was about to go all out. After letting her ride me for a moment, I made her climb off. I put her on all fours, spread her ass wide open ,and spit right in her ass. She looked back at me like she never experienced anything like it, but I wasn't going to let up.

"Bitch, turn yo' ass around. Spit on the tip of my head and suck it up slowly while you look me in the eyes."

As she did what she was told, I grabbed the back of her head and forced my dick down her throat.

"Ahhh...ahhhh." Her eyes popped out her head and tears ran down her face.

Once I felt I was satisfied, I put her back in the same position. I rammed my dick so hard in her ass she cried out loud and tried to run from me, but couldn't because I had my left hand around the back of her neck.

"Truthhhh! Baby, you kill....ohhh, shit, Daddy, don't stop! Please, don't stop!"

I continued to brutally fuck her ass hole like she was a porn star in a Pornhub video. I knew this was what Tasha liked, so I didn't spare her. The way she was begging me not to stop did something to me. I blanked out and showed no mercy. One thing about her, she was a cold freak, and this why she kept my dick hard.

"Ohhhh, just like that! Fuck this ass, Daddy! Fuckkkkk it, Daddy!"

She was screaming so loud I was sure they heard her a mile away. For the rest of the hour, I fucked her in the ass until she couldn't take any more. I slid out slowly as I was nutting and watched my cum ooze out her ass and drip down her pussy lips. I looked at the damage I'd done, and I felt bad for blowing her ass out. I kissed her on both ass cheeks, then smacked it.

I could tell she wasn't getting up, still overdosed, so I got up to grab a towel. I wiped her off, then headed for the shower. Tasha had given me pussy power, so going back to sleep wasn't an option. It was time I hit the streets and get to the bag. I was satisfied, and so was she, so I knew she wouldn't be fucking with me for a few days.

Reign

"She walks the mile makes you smile all the while being true
Don't take for granted the passions that she has for you
You will lose if you chose to refuse to put her first
She will if she can find a man who knows her worth..."

"Sang it, Reign!" Ms. Pearl jumped to her feet and shouted.

Before the song could end, everyone was standing to their feet, clapping. When I spotted Mr. Gary in the audience, I could see his huge smile from the stage. I did my usual bow and exited the stage left, per house rules. I walked over to give Ms. Pearl and gave her a hug as she clapped for Adrian, the next act who was now singing a song by The Temptations. After, I headed over to Mr. Gary, and he bowed along with me.

"You a beast up there, Reign. Where's your guitar?"

"It's home. I need a few dollars so I can restore it. A few of the strings were loose."

"Well, come on by the house. I'll give you a few dollars."

"Oh, no, Mr. G, you've done enough. Thank you." I smiled

at Mr. G, who was actually dressed nicely.

He was wearing a pair of jeans with a button-down and a cowboy hat with boots to match. I couldn't help but laugh when I looked up, and he was checking out the ladies.

"I ain't been here in years. Back in the day, it was a boogie joint. I made a lot of money here betting on horses. They still got that old jukebox." He smiled, and I could tell being here took him down memory lane.

"Where was Mrs. G?"

"Right by my side. Her ass thought every girl wanted me, so she wouldn't let me out her sight. I told her I only had eyes for her, but she ain't wanna listen. Back then, we weren't married, so the moment I took her hand in marriage is when she relaxed. Nobody wanted my ass. Well, I didn't want them because they all wanted Mr. G. Reign, I was a mack, child." He popped his collar like he was young.

I burst out laughing. We began to make small talk about the club, and eventually, Mr. G went to get him a drink, so I took it upon myself to go see Tony.

I headed for Tony's office to let him know I was leaving. Because of my age, he made me promise to always inform him when I was leaving because it was so late. Most times, he would drop me off around the corner, or he'd have, Jean, one of the guards, drive me. Since Mr. G was here, I was gonna catch a ride with him and walk home. I opened the door to Tony's office and walked in to find him. His office was huge, and it had a second level that connected to a studio. Just as I expected, Tony sat behind his equipment thumbing with the keyboard.

"Reign, I want you to hear something." His foot began to bop, and he hit one of the switches on the board. It began to play a pop beat with a guitar line that made me wanna hear more. "Now watch this," he said excitedly and hit a few more buttons that added a slight bass with a melody that sounded familiar. "Bet you don't know that sound?" he asked, and I tried hard to think of it. "Faze-O," he answered before I could.

One thing I knew was some oldies because my mom and all her junky friends used to have my house rocking. They would play cards, smoke their crack, drink all night, and make all the noise in the world. I was young, pissy with a hanging diaper, but I had a ball with the drug addicts. They would always give me candy and even play with me. I could remember this one lady named Franky who always cursed my mother out for not feeding me or leaving me dirty. My mother would always brush her off, too high to focus.

"This sounds good." I began to tap my foot along with him. I looked around the room, and when my eyes landed on the mic inside the booth, I imagined myself inside singing one of my own jams. I didn't have the confidence to do so, so I quickly turned my head and focused on the beat. "Mr. G is here, so I'm gonna catch a ride with him."

"Okay. You be good now. I'll see you next Friday."

"Okay. Maybe I'll swing by sooner and hang out." I smiled and headed for the door.

Tony waved goodbye, and I walked out. I went to find Mr. G because I was now hungry as hell. Lately, when I got hungry, my stomach would start pounding and doing summersaults. Ms. Arnold had made us some breakfast, but that was over fifteen hours ago. I couldn't go another minute without eating. Therefore, I prayed that Mr. Gary had cooked.

"Damn. Hi, friend."

"Heyyy." I giggled as I stepped into Raylen's bedroom.

I knew the sarcastic "*Hi, friend*" was because she hadn't seen me in a minute, and it kinda made me smile. It told me she actually missed me, and the feelings were mutual. Ray had been so busy and private that I tried my best not to get in her way. Not to mention, I was so embarrassed about my weight. When I was home, all I pretty much did was sleep. Therefore, I couldn't be mad because out of insecurity, I kept my distance too. When we bumped heads in the house, we made small talk. I tried to remain supportive about her pregnancy, but whenever conversations were brought up about the baby, she would shy away from the subject. Especially when the subject of a baby daddy was brought up. I wasn't sure if maybe she didn't know who the father was, or was she ashamed it was Devin?

"Where have you been? I hear you back there messing around with that guitar and then you vanish."

"Yeah, I be tryna play, but the strings are loose. Soon as I get a few bucks, I'll get it fixed. Other than that, I'm always down helping Mr. Gary." I smiled with a lie. I didn't know why I just couldn't be upfront with my best friend about the Cabana; especially because she was the one who insisted I go audition.

"Oh, okay. Well, I miss you." She smiled, and I walked further into her bedroom.

I went to take a seat, and I couldn't help but stumble back on her bed. When my rear end hit the mattress, a loud thump could be heard, and the bed sank. I looked over at Raylen, embarrassed that I had broken her bed.

"I'm so sorry, friend." I jumped up and began examining it.

"Reign, it's okay. It's old anyway. Plus, I have to buy a new one for me and the baby."

"Okay." I dropped my head and leaned against the wall.

"Stop looking like that. It was an accident," Raylen tried to assure me.

I nodded my head, and the sudden aura coming from the door made me look over.

"The fuck happen to yo' bed?" Truth walked further into the room.

Instead of Raylen responding, she looked up at me, making Truth's eyes double over in my direction. Again, I dropped my head, and the room got silent.

"Let me get that weed?" Truth asked Raylen, and she rolled her eyes.

I didn't know what her problem was lately, but she had been acting like Truth was the enemy since her pregnancy. I knew women's hormones changed, which was why she was so moody. I just couldn't believe she acted like that with Truth. He hit her with an annoyed glare as she handed him the Ziplock of weed. He then walked out, and I was finally able to breathe.

"Damn, don't pass out on me." Raylen laughed and waved her hand as if she were fanning me.

"That man is fine as hell."

"He a'ight."

"Girl, you must be smoking dicks. He is beyond alright."

"I can't believe you're still in love with him after all this time." She shrugged her shoulders as if she didn't think Truth was all that and a bag of chips.

"Girl, I'll be in love with that man until my dying days." I closed my eyes to savor the moment of my thoughts.

I opened my eyes in just enough time to catch her rolling her eyes again. I ignored her and headed out the door. I went into my bedroom and pulled out my guitar. I began tightening the strings that were definitely gonna come loose again, however, it would be good enough to play. I began playing an Alicia Keys song and imagined myself at the Cabana; only this time, I was famous, and the crowd was there to see me and only me.

Reign

I jumped out of my sleep and rushed to the bathroom. The moment I made it to the toilet, everything I ate last night came rushing from inside of me. I spent so much time in the same spot vomiting I had to take a shower. When I got up from the floor, my body felt so weak, and I knew I had over done it. Last night, Ms. Arnold had made enchiladas, and right after, I scarfed down a chili cheese burger from A1 Burgers. After that, I dug into my bag of snacks Mr. Gary had given me with Twix, Hershey's, and Skittles. Now, here I was paying for it.

I headed into my room and grabbed my clothing, along with my towel. By the time I was back in the hallway, I could hear Truth's voice coming from Raylen's bedroom. I couldn't hear what he was saying, but I could hear yelling. If I didn't know any better, I would think they were more of lovers than fake brother and sister.

I continued on towards the restroom and instantly began undressing. I sprayed a little air freshener because the smell of vomit still reeked. I then took off my top, followed by my shorts, and just as I took off my fake gold chain the door flung open. My heart dropped, and I closed my eyes, knowing it was Rayvon only coming to assault or insult me.

"My bad, Reign."

My eyes flung open to the sound of Truth's voice. Instead of him shutting the door, his eyes ran down my entire body, and he frowned. I already knew what he was thinking. I wrapped my arms around my body, trying hard to cover myself.

"Please go," I whispered, already embarrassed enough.

He nodded once and closed the door behind himself.

I jumped into the shower and that shit disturbed my thoughts. I knew he was probably outside making fun of me right along with Rayvon. I tried hard to forget about it, so I started lathering my towel and soaping my body. After rinsing off, I stepped out and didn't bother drying off. I grabbed my clothing and headed for my room. I quickly slid into my clothes as tears began to fall from my eyes. I thought of the look Truth had plastered on his face and that shit hurt. All I wanted to do was hop into the bed and cry myself to sleep. Because it was only Wednesday, I couldn't go to the Cabana, so I was stuck here in sorrow.

Just as I was climbing into bed, the sound of rapid gun fire erupted. I could hear them clearly as they tapped against the metal stand Ms. Arnold kept in the room. It was like I couldn't move fast enough, and with the fear I felt, I rolled off the bed and crashed into the ground.

"Arhhhhhh!" I let out a loud growl because a pain shot through my body from my stomach to my back.

"Reign, are you okay!" Ms. Arnold asked, busting in.

"I'm fine. I just hurt myself falling from the bed. Is everyone okay?" I asked out of fear that something could have happened to Truth.

"Yes, Truth and Tasha were outside, but they're both okay."

I nodded my head okay, and she disappeared back down the hall. Knowing Truth was okay, I lay back down and tried hard to doze off. Raylen burst into my room in a panic to make sure I was okay. When I told her I was fine, she headed back out the door.

"All alone, on my knees I pray
For the strength to stay away
In and out, out and in you go
I feel your fire
Then I lose my self-control
How can I ease the pain
When I know you're coming back again…"

With every word I sang, I felt faint. I tried hard to keep a straight face, but agony shot through my body, causing me to slightly frown. Everyone in the crowd was jamming to my song of choice, which was Lisa Fischer's "How Can I Ease the Pain." They sang along and moved their bodies side to side.

It was like Mr. Gary and I were chemically combined because he had a worried look on his face. He watched me steadily, and I shrugged my shoulders, gesturing to him that I didn't know what was wrong. I tried hard to continue, but the pain had grown so uncomfortable I stopped to grab my stomach. Suddenly, a gush of liquids came flowing down my legs, confusing me because I didn't have an urge to pee. When I looked down, I noticed blood, and my body became faint.

"Someone call an ambulance!" Was the last thing I heard before I blanked out and everything went black.

"Ms. Paul, if you can hear me, look directly into the light." I heard a voice say, so I looked up, right into a light that made me squinch my eyes.

"Doctor George, her blood pressure is a little high. Vitals are stable for her and the baby."

"Give me the activity for muscle tone and respiration for the baby."

Baby? I thought as I watched the doctor and nurse correspond with one of another. I began looking around the room, and the room was surrounded with small incubators. The sounds of a baby's cry could be heard clearly, and it made me wonder what was going on.

"Hello, Mommy." A female doctor approached me and smiled.

"Mommy?" I asked her as if I didn't hear her clearly.

"Because the baby only weighed one pound, she will have to stay here for a few weeks, or until she gets at least four pounds."

"Wait, what baby are you talking about?" I frowned, ready to cry, because she had to be mistaking me with another patient.

"I'm talking about your baby girl you gave birth to, Ms. Paul. Tomorrow, you will be naming her and signing the birth certificate. Right now, your body is in distress, so you need to get some rest," she said and pulled the sheet up to my chest.

I watched this woman loosely move around my room as if she didn't have a care in the world. I was still in disbelief about this whole baby thing, and she didn't seem to be convincing me or even making me understand where the hell a baby came from.

Finally, I looked down at my bracelet, and it read my name and Baby Paul, along with *gender: female, 1 lbs with 4 ounces.* I studied the bracelet for quite some time before finally accepting the fact that I had given birth.

I began thinking about the last few months and how my body had changed. All that time, I thought I fell into depression and started gaining weight, but that wasn't the case. I was pregnant all along. The more I sat and thought about it, the deeper my thoughts began to overdose. When reality sat in, it all boiled down to me giving birth to a baby who was conceived during a rape. I began shaking my head as tears ran down my face.

I thought of Rayvon's words, and I knew I couldn't show up with a damn baby. That nigga was ruthless, and I knew he would kill me. I just couldn't. I began sobbing harder, thinking about my life. What could I do with a child? A damn unwanted baby at that. I didn't know how to love myself properly, so if I did give the child a chance, I would still fail.

Truth

"What about Fat Bitch?"

"What about her?" I asked.

"Man, you sure always go into defense for that bitch."

"You always got some shit to say about that girl. Anyway, why you say it's her, though?"

Before Rayvon responded, he rolled his eyes like a bitch. "I mean think about it. The bitch always disappearing. Then the day they came through squeezing, she went MIA. Just because you wouldn't fuck her, and I damn sure wouldn't fuck her, don't mean one of our opps won't. They prolly fucked the bitch just to get some info from her." He took a pull from the blunt, then passed it to me.

I didn't even reply because the nigga had a point. It'd been almost a month since they came through shooting. Every day since then, it's been a warzone, and Reign had gone missing. I wasn't playing with these niggas. I was going through knocking them off one by one, and I wasn't gonna stop until I got that nigga Cugo. He was the nigga over there with all the money, and the one that sent his troopers at us. It was like something triggered them off because we hadn't been at war with these niggas in the last two years.

Everything was smooth in the hood, which made the money flow. Now here we were having to watch our backs while we hustled. I hated looking over my shoulders because I had to do that with the police. I knew this shit was gonna go on for the next couple months because eventually, they would surrender after losing too many of their men. In this game, y'all already know; kill or be killed. I wasn't dying. I had a reputation in these streets, and I was definitely untouchable. Because my money was long, I had more choppers than the NY Police Department. I would take they whole hood out effortlessly.

"I'm telling you I don't trust her," Ray added, and again, I ain't reply.

It was like as soon as the war unfolded, Reign just disappeared off the face of the earth. I also thought back on how many weekends she would vanish into the night. She would go missing for hours, then reappear as if it were nothing. I always brushed it off as her having a nigga somewhere, and maybe I was right. The nigga could have been an opp. True, Reign was big and had even put on more pounds, but she wasn't ugly. I've seen skinny bitches who couldn't even fuck with Reign in the looks department. Therefore, it was niggas out here who would definitely look past her weight.

"I'm 'bout to shoot to moms crib for a minute." I gave Ray a pound and headed for my whip. Before I got in I looked back. "You got yo thang on you, right?" I asked him, and he lifted his shirt for me to see the twin Berettas he had strapped to him. I nodded in approval and got into my whip.

I pulled off from the block and headed out to Yorkborough for my mom's crib. As I drove towards the crib, I called Tasha, but her ass ain't answer. I shook my head and dialed her again because she was supposed to be meeting me. Today, moms was cooking a family dinner, so she insisted we come. When Tasha ain't answer for the third time, I sent Mekol a text to meet me for dinner. I knew I was playing it close because Tasha would pull right up, but I ain't give a fuck.

Lately, the bitch seemed so in tune with her friends that she only took my money and used me for my dick. I really ain't trip because a nigga was constantly in the streets. Shit, I barely had time for my mother and father, which was why I made it my business to drop in occasionally for dinner.

Ding!

Raylen: *Where you go?*

I looked down at my phone just as Ray's text came through. Instead of replying, I called her.

"Why what's up?"

"Because I'm asking. Now where you go?"

"I'm on my way to mom's crib for dinner," I answered because I ain't feel like arguing.

"Oh, okay. Well, the last of the weed gone. When you get a chance, drop some off."

"Yeah, a'ight," I replied, and she hung up.

When I pulled up to mom's crib, I dreaded going in because I knew I was gonna have to tell her I had a seed on the way. It wasn't that I was scared; it was the fact that I was having one by Raylen. She knew Raylen really good because, just as Ms. Arnold watched me grow up, my moms watched Raylen grow up too. Her and Ms. Arnold were close friends until I moved my moms and dad away from the hood.

I climbed out my whip and headed inside. As soon as I walked in, my stomach started turning. It smelled good as fuck. Before making my way into the kitchen, I went to find my pops. I walked into his man cave, and he was on the phone.

"Sup, Pops. When you done, can you come here? I need to

holla at you and Moms."

"Hey, son. Okay, give me five mins."

"A'ight." I walked out and began searching for my mother.

"Hey, handsome." She lit up when she saw me.

"Sup, Ma." I kissed her cheek. "It smells good in here, lil' lady."

"That's them greens. You know I can hook up some greens. Where's that girlfriend of yours?" She looked around me, waiting for Tasha.

"She ain't coming. Mekol might pull up, though. Speaking of, I got something I wanna tell you before she gets here."

"Oh, Lord. Spill it."

"I'm waiting on yo' husband."

"Okay." She chuckled.

Moments later, my dad walked in and kissed my mom on the back of the neck. It made me smile seeing how they were still so affectionate, even after all these years. I mean, he did put her through some shit.

"Spill it," my mom said again impatiently.

"I'm 'bout to be a daddy."

"Ohh, son that's good. Is Tasha excited?" my dad asked while my mom frowned.

"It's not by Tasha."

"Well, who's it by?" my mom asked, and I could see the excitement in her eyes. She couldn't stand Tasha fa shit.

"Raylen."

"Raylen? Little Raylen?" she asked, and I nodded.

"When did y'all start fucking?" my pops boldly asked, making me chuckle.

"We not fucking. It happened a couple times, and her ass got pregnant."

"So she's trapping you?" my pops asked, and again, I laughed.

"Nah, Pops. She just wants a baby, I guess."

"Well, does Karen know about it?" Moms asked, referring to Ms. Arnold.

"She know she pregnant, but not by me."

"Well, y'all have to tell her soon. I know that son of hers is gonna be pissed."

"Hell yeah," I agreed because it was true. I thought of that all the time, and every day, I prepared myself to lose a friend.

Reign

"Ms. Paul, are you excited about leaving?"

I watched my nurse walk into my room and pull open the curtains. I didn't reply because hell no; I wasn't excited. I was a prisoner; or, at least that was how I felt. No visits, no contact, nothing. I mean, who was I gonna call? What would I say? Therefore, I had to be prisoned in this hospital bed until Serenity gained the pounds she needed to go home.

It was now two weeks shy of three months since I've been here, and the baby made great progress. She had hit her four pounds, so we were due to leave. The thing was, to where?

I walked over and grabbed Serenity out of her bed and snuggled her close to me. She was still so little, but she had features to die for. I took her little, tiny hands into my finger and stared at her graciously. She had a hair full of jet black hair, a honey-golden complexion, and a pair of lashes to die for. On the side of her eye was a small purple birthmark that resembled a raindrop. It was actually cute because one would mistake it for a mole.

"Don't be nervous, baby. Anything goes wrong, you can always come back. In this bag, I've packed you tons of diapers. Make sure you don't show the front; I'd get in trouble. In this bag are pacifiers, bottles, wipes, and everything you will need. The front desk called you a cab, and they should be down there. I need you to sign here and here. These are your discharge papers." She slid the paper over to me with an ink pen.

I signed the papers and looked over the bags she had packed. "Thank you." I faintly smiled because I could tell she had outdone herself.

I didn't want to seem unappreciative, but I just couldn't help it. She thought shit was a piece of cake, not knowing what I was up against. Since the baby was bundled already, I lifted from the bed sluggishly. I put the baby in the car seat that was given to me by the hospital. I then took a seat in the wheelchair and waited for the nurse to roll me out.

When we made it downstairs, the sun was bright, and it shined through the stained windows. The hospital was busy, and people moved around going on with their busy day. The nurse rolled me to the door, and there was my cab awaiting.

"You take care, Reign," she spoke, calling me by my first name.

I nodded my head and lifted from the chair. I put the baby into the taxi, then climbed in behind her. When the taxi pulled off, I lay my head back, letting my thoughts consume me. This man had the address to Raylen's home, but I couldn't show up there. At least not with this child.

"Hey, my baby
Why you lookin' so down?
Seems like you need a lovin'
Baby you need a girl like me
(around)..."

I began singing with my head still lying back. Finally, building up the strength, I looked down at Serenity, who was sound asleep. A tear that I had been trying so hard to hold back slid down my face, and I quickly wiped it away.

"Stop! Stop right here!" I shouted to the taxi driver and looked around the quiet neighborhood.

When the car came to a halt, I grabbed the car seat and jumped out before he could ask any questions. I threw the diaper bag over my other shoulder and slammed the door shut. I began walking up the street until I was tired, and my body felt as if it would give out. I stopped to take a breath just as the cab passed me by. The driver looked at me, but I didn't make any eye contact with him. I turned my head, and my eyes landed on a nice, little white home with black trimming and a large white angel statue in the front.

"1216," I mumbled the address to myself as I let out a deep sigh. Remembering what I had to do, I quickly opened the gate and ran as fast as I could.

"Hey my baby
Tell me why you cry
Here take my hand and (yeah)
Wipe those tears from your eyes..."

I continued singing the second part of Aaliyah's "I Care 4 U" as a wave of tears began to pour from my eyes. I shook my head side to side, not believing what I was about to do, but I had no choice. I sat Serenity's car seat down on the front porch, along with her diaper bag, and turned to run off. I began running so fast I never even got a chance to stop and look back. I couldn't stop crying, and I knew after this, my heart would never recover. I couldn't stop asking God to forgive me, although I was sure He understood my pain.

I couldn't take that innocent human being to that home. Rayvon would kill me for embarrassing him, and not only that, I wasn't fit to be someone's mother. I just couldn't do it. I couldn't do it. A new set of tears began to pour from my eyes. When I was far away from the home, I finally got a chance to stop. Truthfully, my emotions brought me to a complete halt. All I could do was picture that baby's face and the innocence of her eyes. I thought of my mother and how, for so many years, I felt abandoned. Although I abandoned my child, I couldn't raise her the way Angela raised me. I didn't have shit to my name and that baby deserved better. I prayed to God she got the care she needed and ended up with a family that would love her. This was it; this was the best decision.

"I love you, Serenity," I whispered, looking up to God.

I really did love her; because over this course of time, we got a chance to bond. However, loving her didn't have anything to do with what she deserved. Me loving her was why I made the decision I chose to make. I knew one day, in my heart, I may see her again, and when that day comes, maybe I'd be able to provide and care for her. Who knows?

"Reign! Oh my God! Where have you been! What's wrong! Why you look like that? Reign, are you okay?"

"I'm fine, Ray. I just wanna lie down."

"You wanna lie down? You've been gone almost three months, and you wanna lie down? The fuck?" She placed her hand on her hip.

I knew this wasn't gonna be easy, which was why I didn't wanna come. However, I had no choice. It was here, or a shelter, and right now, I ain't feel like dealing with questions and authorities possibly looking for me. I looked at Ray, and she was grilling me so hard I couldn't do shit but take a seat.

The room went quiet for a moment until I thought of a lie. I mean, this was my best friend, so I couldn't just leave her hanging with no explanation.

"I've been staying down at the Cabana. The owner let me perform for a little change on weekends. He also has a studio upstairs where he let me crash. I got into it with my mom, and she threatened to call 12 on me because I'm technically still a minor. Ray, I couldn't have that heat on y'all, so I decided to lay low for a moment."

*And the Academy award for best acting goes to...*I thought as I looked at Raylen with a straight face and lied through my teeth. When I mentioned the last part about them not catching any heat, her face softened, and she looked more understanding.

"That skank, butch bitch." Ray smashed her fist into her hand.

I finally looked down, and her stomach was huge. "Damn, you big as fuck."

"I'm due any day. I be glad when this shit over so I could get back to my hoe shit. You know when it comes to my hoeing I don't play..." She did a little dance just as Truth walked in.

He looked at Raylen and shook his head, then his eyes zoomed in on me. They danced over my body slowly, and I got nervous, hoping he didn't notice the weight I had lost. My once huge stomach was gone, and due to so much stress, I shed some pounds. After he stalked my body with his eyes, he looked at me and frowned. Normally, his facial expressions were so pleasant, but not now. I took this as my cue to go because really I wanted to get away from Ray before I broke down. I raced out of the room, acting like I had to use the bathroom. I ran straight down the hall at full speed.

"Damn, watch where you going!"

I bumped right into Rayvon's ignorant ass. He was coming

out of his bedroom with a chick behind him. I rolled my eyes, knowing he fucked her in the bed, but I kept it pushing. As soon as I hit the room, just like I knew, it smelled like some bad pussy. I clutched my stomach and grabbed the can of Febreze they failed to use. I began spraying the room, and already, I regretted coming back here. Sigh.

Truth

"Truth, let me get a dime."

I heard my name being called, so I turned around. "Angela, yo' base-head-ass know damn well I don't sell dimes. Go holla at Rayvon." I dismissed her and turned my back to her.

If it was one bitch I hated, it was her. I despised the hoe because of how she did her daughter. She left that girl for dead. Down here with hood niggas wasn't a place for someone like Reign to be. But nah, this bitch chose a nigga and crack over her child. I really ain't know the full details 'bout what happened, but it couldn't be too bad coming from Reign. That girl ain't that bad.

"Shit, here comes her fat ass," Angela mumbled under breath and scurried off up the street where Rayvon was standing.

I looked back, and Reign was coming down the steps wrapped in a brown leather coat and a pair of leggings. She made her way up the street, and if I wasn't tripping, it looked like she was trying to creep. She never even noticed me standing in the cut because I was dressed in all-black, waiting on the opps to call themselves rolling on us. From time to time, she looked back and around to check her surroundings, and it made me think of what Rayvon had said a few months back.

When Reign was out of eyesight, I decided to follow her. I quickly hopped into my whip and made sure my strap was off safety. I began driving but made sure to go as slow as possible. I drove for about twenty minutes and followed Reign onto Broadway. Instead of her walking straight, she turned into a building, and from outside, I could see flashing lights. I wasn't sure if she had gone into the building's door or the Cabana that was attached to an old, deserted apartment building. I threw my car in park and decided to sit here for a moment.

After about thirty minutes, there was no sign of Reign, so I got out and headed to the door. I knew the security and owner of the club, so if Reign went inside, I'd definitely find her.

"Truth, what's up?" I slapped hands with Larry, the security.

"Shit, just coming to check the spot out. Have me a drank."

"Oh, okay. Gone right in." He nodded and let me in without patting me down.

I mean, there wasn't shit going on in the Cabana because this place was filled with old heads.

I stepped further into the club, and I damn near choked from all the cigarette smoke. However, I kept it pushing right inside. The place was dim, but it wouldn't be hard to spot Reign, so my eyes began to roam the club. It was pretty packed, and everyone seemed in tune with the chick on the stage singing.

"How can you mend a broken heart?
How can you stop the rain from falling down?
How can you stop the sun from shining?
What makes the world go round?"

The angelic voice sang a familiar song my mother and

father used to play growing up. But what made me freeze was, the powerful voice that tranquilized the whole club was Reign. I stopped dead in my tracks and listened to her sing that song from her soul. I swear, for a minute, I fell into a daze watching her.

"I Can still feel the breeze that rustles through the trees
And misty memories of days gone by
We could never see tomorrow, no one said a word about the sorrow..."

She had her eyes closed, but the tears on her cheeks were visible. The wrinkles in her forehead made it evident that she felt some sort of pain. When I say this chick had a nigga stuck; it was like I felt every emotion she felt. The song actually took me back to my childhood and that was a memory lane a nigga would never forget.

"Mom, are you okay?"

"Yes, baby I'm fine. Go into your room and watch TV."

"No, you're not. If you're okay, then why are you crying?" I stopped to look at my mother, whose face was buried into her feather goose pillow. The moment she heard my voice, she looked up, and that's when I saw the tears. "Is it my dad? Did Dad make you fall out of love again? If he did, I can make you love again, Ma. I promise."

She looked up at me with her big, beautiful eyes and began to shake her head. "Oh, Truth, you're just a child. What do you know about love?" she asked, and I stopped to find the words.

I was only nine, but I knew about love. I felt love every day from my mother.

"I know a lot about love. I love you. I'll never hurt you like Daddy."

My eyes welled up with tears because I hated seeing her hurt. I mean, my dad was a good dude, but right here in this same room, was where he had done all his dirt. Back then, it was a boogie joint where all the old heads hung. The drug dealers, and even the killers. The heroin addicts and all the side bitches. Plenty of times, I'd ride my bike down here to beg from my pops and his friends, and I'd see everything he was doing. I played dumb because that was what they figured I was: just a dumb child. However, I was no fool. I knew why my mother cried.

The trip part was, the women my pops chased through the hood were scallywag hoes. None of them compared to my moms, and until today, they couldn't hold a candle next to her. I never understood why she stayed, but I guess that was what love did. I knew this was a reason I tried to work shit out with Tasha. My mom never gave up, and I respected her for that.

"Truth, my man!"

I was knocked from my thoughts by Tony, who stood in front of me with his fist in the air for a pound. "Tony, what's up?" I gave him a pound and a manly hug.

He turned to look at the stage, and he began shaking his head. "Good talent gone to waste."

I focused in on Reign, and I nodded my head *yes* without

realizing I was agreeing.

"You know, Truth. I hate to let that poor child down. She comes here every weekend and pours her heart right on that stage."

"But why let her down?" I asked, and he stopped to look around his establishment.

"I can't afford it. The liquor sales are down. I'm barely making enough to pay the bills around here," he responded, and I could see the hurt in his eyes.

Tony had been the owner for over two decades. He wasn't the owner when my parents came here, but he was the second owner shortly after.

"Damn, man, I hate to hear that." I shook my head and looked back at Reign.

She had just finished her song, and everyone stood to their feet to clap for her. This was my cue to slide, so I told Tony I would see him around. Hearing Tony say Reign came every weekend killed the curiosity of her fucking on the enemies. Therefore, my job here was done. I headed out before she could see me and jumped in my car. I pulled off but only around a few blocks. I had a feeling Reign was gonna be walking back home, so I decided to stay behind and give her a ride.

I sat back in my seat, and about twenty minutes later, I could see her walking up the street fast as fuck. I knew she was walking fast because it had begun to lightly drizzle. Because of the dark clouds that hovered over the sky that was another reason I decided to stay. I knew it would eventually rain. I just didn't think it would be that quick. I started my car and pulled up alongside her.

"Reign!" I called her name, and she stopped as if she were unsure it was me. "Man, bring yo' ass on before I leave you in this rain." I put the car in drive like I was gonna really leave her.

She ran over to my whip, and I could tell her ass was nervous because she couldn't even shut the door.

"Man, slam that damn door." I chuckled and pulled off as she closed the door.

As we headed for the block, Reign was quiet the whole time. She was nervous as hell sitting in my passenger seat, and she couldn't stop bouncing her leg.

"Where you coming from?"

"Huh...ummm...oh, a friend's," she stumbled and told a bold face lie.

"A friend, huh?" I chuckled again and kept straight.

I wasn't tryna make her more nervous than she already was. As bad as I wanted to, I let up on her because not only were we pulling up to the crib, but Tasha was sitting out front. I shook my head, knowing it was gonna be some bullshit. Because for some reason, she couldn't stand Reign.

As soon as my whip parked, Tasha was already coming my way. I watched Reign with her sly smirk as if she was taunting her further. I laughed like a muthafucka because it was evident Reign wasn't scared of Tasha.

"Why the fuck this fat hoe in yo car!" she shouted, making sure Reign heard her.

Reign looked back and laughed, but she kept it pushing right to the front door.

"Damn," I cursed because Rayvon was gone, and Reign ain't have a key. Therefore, Raylen had to come unlock the door.

"Truth, I know you fucking hear me! Why is this bitch in yo' fucking car!"

"Man, gon', Tasha. It's raining, so I gave the girl a ride."

"Nigga, that ain't yo' bitch, so it ain't yo' duty to give her no damn rides!" She was bouncing up and down, all extra out.

I then knew she was drunk, and by the way she was dressed, she had been out with her friends. It was below twenty and raining, but that didn't stop "Thot'sha." I swear this was the biggest reason I ain't take that second step with Tasha. Well, one of the reasons, but this was the main one. Her ass didn't know how to sit down and be a girlfriend.

She knew a nigga hustled day in and day out, but she never

called to ask was I hungry. I remember times when she bled the block wit' a nigga, but all that changed. Baby girl traded in her trap clothes for tramp clothes. I mean, I ain't want her out here, but I ain't want her in the club every week either. I needed a wife to stay home, wash a nigga clothes, cook a nigga a meal; but that was the problem. She wasn't a wife. Which was why she was gonna stay in the girlfriend zone.

"Truth, take yo' bitch from in front of here with all that yelling."

I heard Raylen's voice as soon as I stepped out of the car. I let out a soft sigh as soon as I saw Tasha turned around all extra.

"Bitch?"

"Yeah, *bitch*," Raylen challenged. She stepped further out the door, but Reign jumped in her way.

"So, what? You bitches gonna jump me?"

"Girl, we ain't gotta jump you. I'll beat yo' ass myself," Reign threatened, taking me by surprise.

When Tasha got quiet, I knew right then she ain't want it wit' Reign.

"Nah, you prolly try to sit on me." Tasha laughed to give herself some time to walk off.

And that right there told me she definitely didn't want it with Reign. Finally, somebody shut her ass up. I chuckled and moved towards my whip so I could go home.

"Raylen, Reign, take y'all ass in the house," I told them before Raylen said some shit that would shut the whole block down.

I started my whip, and I could feel both Reign and Raylen watching me. I kept my head straight and pulled off. I knew Tasha was right behind me, and I knew I wouldn't hear the end of this tomorrow. Raylen hated Tasha, and being pregnant only made shit worse. I knew when the shit hit the fan it was gonna be devastating. I just prayed it would last long enough for me to figure some shit out.

I mean, I had no choice. This was my seed, and the way I was living, I couldn't let my seed live basic. I mean, I wasn't rich;

yet. But a nigga had long money. I had plenty of cars and a five-bedroom out the way. I slept good and comfortably every night, so I was gonna have to arrange for my seed to come home. Somehow, some way.

Reign

"What have you done to me
I can't eat, I cannot sleep
And I'm not the same anymore, no, no
I don't know what to do
'Cause all of me wants all of you
Do I stand alone at the shore..."

It was the same crowd and same energy in the club. However, I was feeling a lot better nowadays. It had still been hard for me to process abandoning my child, but after praying to God and understanding I did what was best for the baby, I've been in a better head space. Not to mention, Truth had been hanging around more and was even being nice to me.

A few weeks ago, when he gave me a ride, I damn near lost it. The whole way home, I was a nervous wreck, but he made me loosen up. Ever since that day, he had been hanging around Raylen and me much more. He even gave me a ride to the store one day he saw me walking in the rain again.

I was sure Truth didn't know what he did to my body and

soul, and this was the reason I was singing this song. I closed my eyes and imagined it was him I was singing to, so it made the song much more intense. By the time I was done, I felt good and had a huge smile. I could tell by the looks of the crowd I had touched a few people because not only were they standing to their feet, but they matched my energy. Normally, everyone looked so gloomy, and I was sure my energy and songs played a big part; and today, all that changed.

I walked off the stage and headed over to Mr. Gary, and of course, his ass was being all extra out with his whistling. I couldn't help but giggle because Mr. Gary had already asked me if I met a new boy. Of course, I denied it because he would die if he knew Truth was the man I was crushing on. I never admitted to Mr. Gary my feelings for Truth because he never had anything good to say about him.

"Oh, Mr. Gary, you so extra." I laughed, playfully hitting him.

"Once again, you did great. Now let's go. I'm hungry."

"I'm gonna stay behind. Tony wanted to see me."

"Okay. I can wait if you need me to."

"No, it's okay. Love you, Mr. Gary."

"Love you too."

Mr. Gary walked off, so I headed for Tony's office. When I walked in, it took me by surprise to find him behind his desk instead of fumbling with the machines to his studio. The papers he was holding he dropped and looked up at me. He had this distant look on his face I couldn't read, and I knew that look too well. It was the same look he gave me when he saw that I was a minor inside his club. Only this time, he looked more sad as if it were bothering him.

"Hey, Tony," I spoke nervously as I closed the door behind me.

"Hey, Reign. I have a seat." He scratched his head, and this really made me curious.

"Tony, I can tell something is bothering you. Can you spill it already because this suspense shit driving me crazy."

He looked at me and removed his glasses. "I have some bad news. Reign, you know I've been in this business over twenty years. Watching you guys perform brightens my rainy days, and boy, I have some rainy days."

"Tony, skip the bullshit." I stood to my feet frustrated with him beating around the bush.

"The club is closing soon."

"What you mean?"

"I mean, the club is closing. I can't afford this place."

"You can't..." I sat back down and looked at him. "Tony, this place means a lot to me. This place is all I have." Tears threatened to fall.

"I'm sorry," he spoke above a whisper and shook his head.

"We have to figure something out. We can't just give up. What if I do fundraisers or bigger events? I mean, something."

"You're still a minor, Reign. You're not supposed to even be here. I'm sorry." He shrugged his shoulders.

It was like Tony was just giving up. When I saw there was no reasoning, I got up to leave.

"Maybe the person who buys this place would keep it as a club. Reign, you'll be eighteen very soon, so you'll be okay."

I nodded my head and couldn't help the tears. I closed the door and headed out of the Cabana. Right now, I felt like *The Dramatics*. All I wanted to do was go outside in the rain. I wanted to mask my tears so no one would see me cry. It was still pouring down rain and had been for the last couple weeks. I ran out of the Cabana at full speed. I didn't bother to respond to Larry, who was calling my name.

"Happy birthdaaaaaay!" Raylen burst into my room, screaming to the top of her lungs.

Her mother was right behind her with a big, goofy smile, so it made me smile and realize I had people who actually cared about my special day.

"Happy Birthday, baby."

"Thank you, Ms. Arnold. Thanks, best friend."

"I made you a cake, and Ray has something for you." Ms. Arnold handed me a chocolate cake with a candle that said *18*.

I took the cake and thanked her. When I looked down, I couldn't help but laugh because Ray had a guitar wrapped up. The shape of the gift was hella obvious, so I laughed at the thought of her wrapping it up.

"Here you go, best friend." She handed me the guitar, and I tore it open.

"Aww, thank you." I looked from the guitar to Raylen, then back to the guitar.

"It was your old guitar. I just got it restored," she said.

I looked in the corner, and sure enough, my guitar had been missing. There was no telling how long because the last couple weeks I've been out of it.

The guitar was dope as hell. It was a sleek purple that had so much shine. On the front was my name with a small thunderbolt underneath.

"Purple Reign," Raylen mumbled, making me smile. It was very unique and dope as hell.

"This dope. I really appreciate you guys." I stepped over to give them another hug, but Ms. Arnold held her hand up.

"Raylen, oh my God!" she shouted hysterically, making Ray and me look down. There was a pool of water flowing from Raylen's legs, and I knew that gush all too well.

"She's in labor. Her water just broke." I tried to remain

calm as I looked at Ms. Arnold.

"Oh my God. I'm scared." Raylen frowned.

"Don't be. You and the baby will be okay." I rushed into her bedroom and grabbed the diaper bag that was already packed. "Ray, get yourself together. It's time," I told her as she emerged from the back room.

When she went into her bedroom to slide into her clothing, I ran into the restroom and slid into some sweats and a tee. My hair was done, thanks to Raylen, so I brushed it down and began brushing my teeth. Once we were all done, we hopped into Ms. Arnold's car and headed for the hospital. This was gonna be a long day, but the thought of my nephew being born on my birthday was a gift. However, it made me think of Serenity, and of course, my day had become gloomy.

Truth

"Aye, bro, I'm finna head to the hospital."

"The fuck wrong with you?"

"Shit. Ray went into labor this morning. She seven centimeters now."

"Word?" I paused, not really knowing how to react. "I'm pulling up right now. Come out. I'mma slide you up there."

"Oh, fasho." He hung up.

Just as I was pulling up, he was coming out the door. I knew I was playing with fire, but because the baby was so little, I was sure he wouldn't have had features. By the time baby Tru turned six months, I was gonna definitely have to break the news. I was gonna tear their family apart, hurt Tasha, and my nigga, Rayvon, wasn't gonna fuck with me. I ain't have a choice because my dumb ass fucked her, she got pregnant, and we had to own up to it as adults.

"I hope her punk ass baby daddy shows up." Rayvon nodded his head as he tapped his pistol that was on his side.

Her baby daddy is showing up, I thought as I kept my head straight.

When we pulled up, Rayvon barley gave a nigga a chance to park. He jumped out, and I wasn't sure if he was eager to see if his sister was okay, or was he really tryna see if the baby daddy was here.

I parked and headed into the hospital. After we were given our passes, we headed up to labor and delivery. As soon as we stepped off the elevators, the first person we ran into was Reign. She was sitting on the bench, and I could tell she was stressed out. I took a seat by her and let Rayvon go inside.

"How far along?"

"She's eight centimeters now," she replied and sighed.

"Why you sound so stressed out? She's gon' be straight."

"I don't know. Labor is just scary, I guess." She shrugged, but I could tell more was on her mind.

Lately, I had been getting Reign to open up more. She still didn't know I watched her perform at the Cabana, and a part of me felt like a creep. I would creep in and creep out like a thief in the night. It was like hearing Reign sing has become an addiction for me. It made me look at her in another light, and keep shit gutta, the songs she chose to sing somewhat attracted me to her.

"Well, it's almost time. After this, we can head home and celebrate your birthday," Ms. Arnold said as she walked over to Reign.

It's her birthday? I thought because she hadn't mentioned it.

"I'm okay, Ms. Arnold." Reign stood to her feet.

We all headed into the room, and as soon as I walked in, Ray looked at me. She was sweating bullets, and just when I thought she was okay, a contraction hit, and she burst out into tears. I wanted so badly to console her ,but I couldn't make it obvious. Rayvon ran to her side, along with Reign, so I stood back to watch. Shortly after, a medical staff ran inside the room, so I assumed it was time.

They all crowded around Raylen and began prepping her for birth. I stood back and watched as they began to coach Ray into delivering.

An hour later, I had a baby boy who weighed seven pounds. I actually got a chance to hold him, but it did fuck me up when Reign cut the umbilical cord. That was supposed to be me, but Reign was good enough. I watched the baby the entire time, and he was cute as hell. He was gonna be a charmer like his dad.

"Come on, Reign." I stuck my head in the door of Reign's bedroom.

She looked up at me stunned because I caught her off guard. "Ummm, where we going?"

"Just get up. It's yo' b-day. We can grab something to eat," I told her and walked out the room to give her a chance to get herself together.

I went outside and got into my whip to wait for her. When she came out, she was dressed simple in some black tights and a purple sweater. She nervously climbed into the car and put on her seat belt. We pulled off towards the Manhattan of Camarillo restaurant.

When we pulled up, I helped Reign get out of the car, and we went inside. I could tell she was a little embarrassed because of her clothing, so I grabbed her hand to make her loosen up. She looked at me again with her big, pretty ass eyes, and again, she was nervous. I couldn't front; Reign was beautiful as fuck, but she let her weight fuck wit' her mental. Over the course of a few months, she had lost tons of weight, and it was looking good on her. She had a fat ass with some thick ass thighs, and to my surprise, her waist was smaller than it appeared.

"Get whatever you want, Reign."

"Okay." She grabbed the menu and began browsing.

"Stop being nervous around me. I'm a cool nigga."

"I'm not...I'm not nervous," she began stuttering as she fumbled with the menu.

"Yeah, a'ight. So tell me about you, Reign. Like, what type of shit you like to do?"

"Umm, I don't know. Sing." She looked up at me as if she thought I would think singing was corny.

"Word? You know how to sing?"

"Yeah, a little."

"Sing something for me."

"Nooooo." She giggled shyly. "I don't sing for people. Only in my bedroom," she told a bold face lie.

"Yeah, a'ight." I chuckled. "So what's up with you and yo' ma dukes?"

"Angela?" she asked, puzzled that I asked.

"Yeah, Angela."

"I don't know. She's weird as fuck," she spoke, and a sense of sadness came over her. "Her boyfriend and I had a fight, so she kicked me out. If you're wondering, I had nowhere else to go and that's how I ended up at Raylen's."

"Oh, okay. Yeah, that's fucked up. Yo' moms a cold bitch, excuse my French."

"You good. Shit, I know. I had to deal with her shit for damn near eighteen years."

"Well, you don't have to anymore. Ms. Arnold ain't trippin off you being there."

"I know, but I'mma leave soon. I'mma go to college and find a job. I been waiting for the day I turned eighteen," she replied and let out a deep sigh.

"What you planning on taking?"

"Honestly, I don't know. I—" she went to say, but the

waiter walked over to take our order.

We placed our orders and continued our conversation. I learned a lot about Reign, and she was starting to pique my interest. She was cool as hell and actually had a goofy personality that I was bringing out of her. I wanted so badly to tell her I loved her voice, but I didn't wanna seem like a creep. She asked me a few questions and even asked about Tasha and me. By the time I was done explaining shit to her, she understood.

For the rest of the night, we laughed, and she loosened up. I liked Reign Paul, and the way I was feeling, I was glad she had joined a nigga.

Reign

"Your energy, feels so damn good to me
It picks me up don't wanna come down
You got me spinning all around (oh) yeah
You need to know, I've got somebody
But, you're beautiful, shh
But still it ain't that type of party now..."

I didn't know why I chose this song, but I could tell everyone was stunned. They were so used to me singing these sad love songs; I switched up the energy in the club. I even had a smile while singing, and everyone was smiling along.

When I looked up, Truth was standing by the bar, and my heart dropped. I almost got choked up, but I continued on, and for some reason, I couldn't take my eyes off him. To my surprise, he watched me, and he made me more nervous. By the time I was done, I had to practically break our eye contact. Ever since the night he had taken me out for my birthday, he had been all in my personal space. I knew it was because he felt sorry for me. I mean, why else would a man like Truth be around?

He would always come into my bedroom and chit-chat with me. I couldn't front, though; that night in the restaurant was deep. I actually opened up to him. Raylen and the baby still hadn't come home, so I didn't expect him to be around as much. Normally, he conducted his business with Ray, and from what I could see, that was why he spent so much time in and out of her bedroom. I'd be lying if I said I wasn't enjoying his company, but he needed to stop. I was beginning to become attached to his presence, and I didn't wanna get hurt.

Now here he was, in my space again. The Cabana was the last place I wanted to see anyone from the neighborhood.

Every time Truth picked me up, I would lie and say I was at my friend's. A few times, he would ask if it was one of my lil' nigga's house, and I'd reply with it wasn't his business. Welp, my secret was up. I was an old Cabana bum like the rest of 'em.

I walked off the stage and bumped right into Tony. I still wasn't feeling him because of him selling the club, and from the night he broke the news to me, I had been avoiding him.

"Reign! I need to see you." He waved me over, and I rolled my eyes.

I walked over to Tony, and I made sure to give him my nonchalant attitude.

"Look, I know you're still upset. That's what I wanted to talk to you about. I have some good and bad news."

"Cut the shit, Tony." I sighed and focused my attention elsewhere dismissively.

"Well, the bad news is, I won't be able to hear that beautiful voice. I'm so sorry, Reign, and I'm gonna miss you."

I turned to look at him while he spoke, and he looked sincere. It made me feel bad because I was being selfish. I couldn't run Tony's program or dictate what this man had going on; therefore, I looked at him and smiled.

"Thanks for everything, Tony. And I'm sorry. It's just, you guys have become a family to me. You, the girls, and the crowd is all I have."

"I understand. Well, the good news is, I found a buyer. He's really interested in you, so he wants to make you a star. He's gonna buy the entire club and the studio." Tony smiled a wide grin.

I didn't know how to feel because Tony knew damn well I was scared to get into that studio booth. He had asked numerous times if I wanted to record, and I'd always tell him no.

"Who is it?" I asked eagerly.

Over the last few weeks, I had been contemplating with myself about recording, but Tony didn't know that.

"Come right this way so you can meet him." He pulled me by the arm and walked me over nearby where Truth was standing.

"Truth, this is Reign, your star. Reign, this is your new boss," Toni introduced us, and my heart dropped.

"How you doing, ma?" Truth extended his hand, and the way he licked his lips followed by the *ma* made my panties wet.

"Hi...hellooo...Umm, nice to meet you." I faked a smile.

I was still ecstatic about him buying the Cabana, but I couldn't show it. He and Tony began speaking to one another, and I was so out of it I didn't realize Tony walked away to give us some privacy. What Tony didn't know was, I knew Truth, and I knew Truth too damn well. He was now my boss, and my secret crush. Tony introduced us like it was nothing, and little did he know, Truth was the man I was singing about.

"So you brought the Cabana?" I asked as if I didn't know.

"Yeah, it's all me, Reign." He smiled, making my heart sink further into my gut. "I hope you ready because I'm about to make you a star." He spoke as if it was just that easy.

Little did I know, it was definitely that easy, and in six months, this man put me on a platform I would have never expected.

"Come on, Reign. Three more shorty," Truth spoke as if he were my trainer.

"Ahhh, ahhhh, ahhhhh."

The trainer blew his whistle, and I damn near collapsed. Truth walked over to me and handed me a bottled water. He looked at Michael, the trainer, with the same look had given him anytime he would come to pick me up. Truth couldn't stand Michael, and I was sure it was because we flirted. Michael was fine as hell, and I mean, what did Truth expect? We spent every day together. Truth always told me that a man was the last thing I needed right now because I needed to focus on my career. I mean, I understood where he was coming from, but quiet as kept, I think it was time.

You heard right. I was being too hot and bothered these days, and I was ready to give my pussy to somebody. I was supposed to be a virgin, but thanks to Rayvon, he had robbed me of that. I wasn't sure if Michael was the man I wanted to give it to, but I knew I was ready.

The reason I liked Michael was not only his looks, but he showed interest in me since the first day he was hired to be my instructor. Therefore, big or small, I knew he liked me. Since the day Truth signed the papers to the Cabana, he's been on my ass about working out and getting in shape for my shows. I was doing shows all over the entire state and even a few out of town. They were small-time shows, but it felt good to see my name next to some top artists.

At times, I would sing oldies, but for the most part, I was now writing and recording my own music. I performed a few songs with my guitar, and anytime I did that, I'd gain the satisfaction of the crowd. One time, I opened up for singer H.E.R., and she told me she heard me sing her song and that I did good. "Damage" was one of my favorite songs, so I sang it every chance

I got.

"You wanna give me another lap?" Michael walked over and asked.

"Sure—"

"Nah, she's done for the day," Truth intervened and tossed me a towel.

This meant to wrap myself up because I was wearing some biker shorts and a crop. Michael looked from Truth to me as if I would challenge him, but I didn't. I shrugged my shoulders because I wasn't gonna dare go against Truth. I wrapped the towel around myself and headed towards the gym's restroom to shower. Before I could make it inside, Truth called out to me.

"Shower at the crib. Grab yo' stuff," he said, and I made a beeline.

I swear if I didn't know any better, I'd think Truth was jealous. It wasn't just Michael he tripped off of. Any man who looked my way, Truth would go crazy. No matter how professional we were or needed to remain, he ain't give two fucks. The hood nigga always came out of him. Everywhere we went, he kept a couple pistols, and he marched around town as my bodyguard and not just my manager.

The shit was sexy at times, until like now, when I wanted Michael all in my space. Hell, Truth needed to understand I liked Michael, and I was ready to get fucked. Tonight was gonna be the night I told his ass. He needed to chill and let me do me. I was human, and, shit, he got pussy regularly.

Tasha's hoe ass was still around, although Truth ain't pay her too much attention. At times, she would come to my shows, and I knew it was only to watch Truth. Granted, I was madly in love with her man, but I respected her enough not to make any moves or disrespect her. Not that Truth was into me or anything.

It was the same shit as six months ago. He was here, in my space, and the only difference was, we were making a few dollars with the music. For each show I did, I got paid five grand. Truth would take fifty percent of my earnings and put $1,000 into my savings and keep $1,500 for himself, which was thirty percent his pay. The other $2,500 he would let me do as I pleased, so I pretty much spent it on designer clothing. Finally, it felt good to be able to buy myself a decent pair of shoes. I didn't go to crazy, but I did splurge on myself a bit.

I couldn't thank Truth enough. In only six months, I had come a long way. I still wasn't making money like the celebrities, but it felt good to hear people singing my songs in the crowd.

"What's the attitude for?" Truth asked the moment we got into his car.

I slammed my door and looked at him as if he had lost his mind. "I don't have an attitude."

"Man, I ain't dumb I know when—" he went to say, but his phone rang. *Wife* popped up on the screen, and it made me roll my eyes. He shook his head and looked from me to the call, then answered. "Yeah?"

"Where are you?"

"On my way to the crib. Why, what's up?"

"Ain't shit up. Just seeing where the fuck you at. I'll be there. We leaving Lit right now."

"A'ight," Truth responded, then hung up.

Again, I rolled my eyes. This what the fuck I was talking about.

"That's my problem. Truth, you have somebody." I turned in my seat to face him. "I'm a grown woman. I'm not a child anymore."

"The fuck that's suppose to mean?"

"It means I want someone too. You know me and Michael —" Before I could even get Michaels name all the way out my mouth, the car swerved. I had to hold on for dear life until I realized we weren't in a near accident; Truth nearly killed us himself.

"So what you saying, Reign? You like dude?"

"I'm saying I just wanna—"

"You wanna, what? Get some dick? Huh! Don't get quiet now!"

"No, I'm not saying I wanna fuck him, but if it happens, it happens. Truth, you got a bitch. Keep shit real, you got a few bitches. Mekol, Tracy, and don't let me forget the little white bitch, Selina."

"What the fuck them hoes got to do with you?"

"Nothing, and what my pussy got to do with you?" I replied smartly.

This nigga had me twisted. Just as I went to speak, his phone rang again. He looked at it, and I could tell he wasn't gonna answer it. I knew it was prolly one of his little hoes, and this only pissed me off more.

"Hello!" I pushed the green button for him and answered. I knew I was being petty, but I ain't care. Nigga wanted to be in my business, so it was time I be in his.

"Reign?"

I heard my best friend's voice on the other end. I looked at Truth, and he had this dumb ass look on his face.

"Hey, Ray."

"Why you sound like that, and where is Truth?" she asked, and I could hear Tru crying in the background.

"He's right here." I looked at him and rolled my eyes.

"What's up, Raylen?"

"You need to come on. The work gone." She spoke with so much attitude and hung up.

Truth didn't look at me, but I could tell he was annoyed by her call. It made me wonder what was up. It seemed like she had been so irritated with Truth lately. A few times, I caught them arguing, and even a few times, I snuck to look on his phone after a heated argument, and it was this same *RL* number. Now it confirmed who it was.

"Why do y'all always act like y'all hate each other? I mean, that's crazy for y'all to be brother and sister."

"Brother and sister shit, I guess." He shrugged and changed the subject fast. "So you like ol' boy?" he asked, referring to Michael.

I nodded my head *yes,* and for some reason, I was scared.

"A'ight." He nodded once and threw the car in drive.

For a couple miles he was silent, and I hated when he did this.

"Truth, I don't get it. Why can't I find someone to love me like you got? I've never in my life had a man who loved me, or anyone for that matter. I wanna be loved. I wanna go on cute little dates," I spoke, and he kept his head straight.

When I looked up, we were heading for my home, and I knew he was mad. Normally, when he said I could shower at the house, he spoke on his house. Truth knew what he was doing. Tasha had already said she was on her way, so he was gonna use being mad to drop me off.

"Stop right here," I told him as he was passing up Mr. Gary's house.

When he stopped, I jumped out and slammed the door. I could feel him watching me, but I never turned around. I ducked off into the building and began knocking on Mr. Gary's door. I really wasn't in the mood to deal with everyone up the street.

When he opened the door, he must have already known it was me because it opened, and no one was right there. I walked in and locked the door behind me. Mr. Gary was standing in the kitchen making a cup of coffee. I watched him as he poured a second cup and slid it across the counter.

"What's wrong with my superstar?" he asked, looking over in my direction.

"How do you know something is wrong?"

"Reign, your energy lately has been so great. You always loud and ghetto." We both laughed. "It's not a bad thing; it just means you're in a great mood. Now look at you today. You damn near whispering. Now who did it to my baby?"

"Nobody, really." I sighed, and he looked at me. For the first time, I was gonna keep shit real with Mr. Gary. I couldn't help it because I damn sure couldn't be real with my best friend. These days, it seemed like Mr. Gary was all I had to talk to. "Truth," I replied and dropped my head.

"Got dammit, Reign." He smashed his hand into the counter. I knew he was disappointed in me, but he was gonna tell me the real. "Did you sleep with him?"

"No, sir."

"But you are?"

"No, of course, not. It's just, there's this boy I like named Michael."

"The trainer," Mr. Gary added, already knowing about Michael.

I nodded my head *yes*. "Well, I wanna do the…you know.."

"Stanky leg?"

"Mr. Gary, what the hell you know about the stanky leg?" I burst out into a fit of laughter.

Before I could continue, someone began banging at the door. Mr. Gary and I looked at one another, but we didn't move. When the person didn't go away, I headed to the door because I was sure it wasn't anyone but Truth. I opened the door without looking, and Angela stepped in.

"Look who we have here. If it ain't the big super star," she taunted. "Fat bitch lost a little weight too." She walked around me in a circle, checking me out.

"Gon' and get yo' ass outta here, hoe!" Mr. Gary shouted from over by the counter.

"Shut yo' old ass up." She flicked him off and looked back at me.

"Angela, what you want?"

"I want you to pay mother support, bitch. I know you got some money. You fucking on that high-roller up the street."

I frowned my face, wondering what the hell was she talking about.

"Oh, don't look like that. The whole neighborhood is talking about it. Word around town, he fucked you before you turned eighteen too."

"I ain't fucking him. I never fucked him."

"Yeah, that's what yo' mouth says. I knew you were a little hoe. Greg didn't lie about you coming on to him."

"Don't nobody want yo' dirty ass, crackhead boyfriend!" I yelled, ready to get mad.

"That's enough, Angela! Get the hell out of my house before I call the police!" Mr. Gary continued to shout.

"Gon' ahead so I can tell them you was fucking a minor too. All y'all niggas nasty." She headed for the door, but I knew she wasn't done.

"Did you tell her you fucked this 'nasty hoe'? Tell her, Mr. Gary."

"Bitch, you get yo' ass..." Mr. Gary jumped to his feet.

I've never seen him move so fast, and it was something about what she said that didn't sit right with him. He slammed the door, and I could hear Angela's laughter. I looked at Mr. Gary, and he remained quiet. I wanted so badly to ask him was there any truth behind what she said, but I left it alone. If he wanted me to know, he would tell me. Now that Angela basically told, I knew sooner or later he would confess to it if it were true.

18

Reign

A few days went by, and I hadn't heard from Truth. I called his phone, but each time, I got no answer. I knew he was in his feelings, but I didn't think it was that bad. A part of me was missing him and ready to go crazy. I would say it was because work needed to get done, and I still had to work out. He hadn't showed up to my training sessions, so for the last few days, Michael had to pick me up.

I really didn't mind because we would drive around the city after. For the first time, in a while, I felt free. However, I did miss Truth. I missed him so much I swallowed my pride and knocked on Raylen's door.

"Come in!" she yelled on the other side of the door.

I opened the door, and she sat on the bed with Tru in between her legs. She was combing his hair, and he was swarming, trying to get out of her reach. The moment he saw me, he reached out for me. I was hesitant for a moment, but I couldn't ignore his cry for me. I rescued my God son from his mother, and he instantly stopped crying.

Raylen watched as Tru and me bonded. I knew she was

shocked that I had come in and grabbed him because I always used my music to act busy. Truth be told, I wasn't too busy. I craved this baby, but I just couldn't do it. After what I had done to Serenity, I just couldn't bond with my G Baby the way I wanted to. The guilt wouldn't let me.

"Umm, have you seen or spoken to Truth?" I asked because I wanted to hand her the baby and quickly leave the room.

"Last night he called about his work. Why, you haven't talked to him?"

"No, he's been ignoring me. Some stuff about a show I flaked on." I shrugged as if it was nothing.

I lied, of course, because I didn't wanna look like a damn fool. My best friend knew I was in love with Truth, but it was strictly business.

"Have you guys, ummm...you know?"

"Ohhh, noooo," I replied and lay Tru down on the bed.

He had nearly fallen asleep, and this would give her a chance to finish his hair. I looked at Ray, and it was something about the look on her face. Maybe she was upset because we were best friends, and she thought I was holding out on her. Whatever the case was, she didn't look too pleased.

"Can I borrow your phone?" I asked, and she looked at me.

She had this hesitant look on her face, but she handed me the phone. I went into her contacts and typed in Truth. His number popped up, so I pushed send and waited for him to answer.

"Sup, Ray?"

"Umm...it's Reign. Where are you?"

"I'm busy. What's up, Reign?"

Raylen and I looked at the phone in disbelief.

"We have work to do, and I have a session at three-thirty."

"Yo' boyfriend couldn't pick you up?" he asked, trying to be sarcastic.

I swear he was lucky Ray was right here.

"No, he said he couldn't today."

"Yeah, a'ight." He chuckled.

I looked at Raylen to see if she had picked up on the sarcastic conversation. She was busy watching Tru. When he disconnected the phone, I took it as he was gonna pick me up. I handed Raylen back the phone and just sat with her in silence.

"So how's the superstar life treating you?" she asked, and it made me look over at her.

It was like that was all everyone called me these days, and it was kinda getting annoying. I was the same ol' Reign and was still trying to make a name for myself.

"It's cool. I'm still tryna get out there. Truth been doing good with booking shows, but I wanna do more. I need the world to know me, so I can have my own show."

"Don't worry. Your time is coming."

"When you coming to a show? You've been in here cooped up with this baby. Yo' ass need to get out."

"I know. I'll go to the one you're having at the arena."

I nodded my head *okay,* and I lifted to leave. "I'll be back to see you guys."

"Okay," she responded with a head nod.

I walked out of the room and towards the living room. Miesha was on the sofa with her and Rayvon's oldest daughter. I swear every time I looked at the little girl, she looked so much like Serenity; it was sorrowful. I quickly turned my head, and Rayvon came walking through the door. He looked me up and down, then plopped down on the sofa.

"Yo fat ass been losing weight. I see you, Reign." He laughed, and, of course, Miesha laughed along with him.

Like always, I ignored the two of them lifeless muthafuckas and went outside to get some air. I looked down at my watch and knew Truth would be coming at any moment. It was almost two p.m., and I had to meet Michael at the gym at three o'clock.

The sound of loud music coming up the street made me scared to turn around. I knew it was Truth because he was just disrespectful when it came to his music blaring. When his car pulled up in front of the building, I headed inside to get my bag.

By the time I came back, he was already out of the car, talking to Rayvon and a few other dudes who were off to the side shooting dice. I rolled my eyes and climbed into Truth's car. I knew Rayvon had some slick shit to say, so I made sure to roll my window up.

Lately, his jokes eased up a little, and I knew it was because I had lost a tremendous amount of weight. I actually noticed him checking me out a few times, and it grossed me out. I was still waiting on his karma to bite him in the ass, and if it wasn't karma, the devil would deal with his ass.

I sat in the car for a few minutes before Truth decided to join me. When he climbed in, he pulled off, and we weren't even two blocks away before Tasha was calling.

"Yeah?"

"Truth, you on the block?"

"Yeah." He looked at me as he lied to his girlfriend.

I turned my head to look the other way because it wasn't my business. She quickly hung up, and we headed uptown for the gym.

When we pulled up, I still hadn't said two words to Truth. I climbed out of the car and snatched my bag up from the backseat.

"Be ready at four-thirty," he said, and I ignored him.

I went into the gym to meet Michael and began my work out. I didn't know why, but through my entire secession, my mind was all over the place. Truth had definitely taken my energy by the way he was acting.

"Reign, you good, love?" Michael asked, looking me in the eyes.

"Yes, Tru...I mean, Michael." I dropped my head annoyed at my clumsiness.

"It's a'ight." He chuckled and walked further to me. "It's obvious you are in love with him, so stop fronting. Reign, that nigga feeling you just as much, so both y'all can cut the shit."

"I'm not feeling him, Michael," I lied but him saying Truth was feeling me did grab my attention. "Truth doesn't want me." I playfully rolled my eyes and looked down at my watch.

I tried hard to ignore the fact that it was an hour past time, and he still hadn't come, however, I was in the company of Michael, and he was always great company. With Michael, it was like I could be myself. He didn't judge me, and he wasn't hyped about my rise in the industry. I could tell he liked me for me and that shit made me love being in his presence.

"And how do you figure?" Michael asked just as I looked up. "Look, Reign. I like you, but I can't compete with a man like Truth. Not only is he some huge drug lord, but the way you look at him alone tells me that's where your heart is. I ain't in no position to lose my life behind a chick who's in love with another man."

"I don't look at him like shit. Michael, I don't want that man. I really like you, and if we can—"

"Reign!"

I heard my name being called, and by the bass in his voice, I didn't have to turn around to not only see it was Truth, but to see his attitude; I heard it all in his roar.

"Get yo' shit so we can go. Now!" He mugged Michael, then looked back at me.

I thought of what Michael said about losing his life, and I could see the timid look all over his face, therefore, I just got up. I walked over to the locker to get my gym bag, and Truth was heavy on my heels.

"The fuck you smacking yo' lips for? You wanna stay with

the nigga 'cause I'll leave you here."

"You could've been said that. Shit, you an hour and a half late. You could've left me right here with Michael." I rolled my eyes and popped my neck. I stopped walking to let him know he could do just that.

He looked at me as if I had lost my damn mind, and before I knew it, I was yoked up against the lockers.

"Everything is a muthafucking game to you!" He roared with a clenched jaw.

He looked me in the eyes, daring me to say some slick shit, but how could I? This man had my big ass off my feet with the look of death in his eyes. His chest heaved up and down, and just like that, I had him pissed.

"What do you want from me, Truth?" was all I could muster up.

Tears threatened to fall from my eyes because this man had me spinning. His mixed signals and deranged emotions were starting to really intervene with my daily living. He continued to look at me, and his face slightly softened. He let out a soft sigh that he clearly didn't know I heard, however, he ain't let me down. Instead, he bent down to place a kiss on my lips and that shit blew me back. I closed my eyes, and I swear the sweet melodies of a song began to play. I didn't know what song, but something soft and sensual with violins cascaded through the air, and I felt like the girls in the movies.

When it came to Truth, my imagination ran wild. This man had me woozy and trapped under his spell. I guess today was the day I submissively let him know because I let him kiss me, and when he stopped to look at me, a pool of tears came crashing down my face. I wanted this moment to last forever, but it didn't because he looked at me and that hardcore exterior came back.

"Somebody shot up the block. Rayvon got hit."

"Oh, no." I covered my mouth.

Although I hated him, I didn't wish death on anyone. I

began to move quickly, and Truth walked out. I sighed softly, still hung up on that kiss. I headed behind him, and I sighed again, now frustrated because once again, I let Truth take me there.

Reign

"Come on, Reign, let's roll," Truth spoke, making me look up.

I looked at Raylen, who sat on the opposite side of the hospital bench. She was busy scrolling on her phone, but when Truth spoke, she stopped. She looked at him and then us, and I swear she had a weird look on her face. I got up from my seat sluggishly because I was tired as hell. It was now 3:42 in the morning, and I had no energy for Truth or Raylen.

We had been at the hospital all day. Truth left and had come back, and if this nigga thought I was a fool, I wasn't. The specs of blood on his Timbs boots stood out to me, and the back of his white-tee had a few splatters of blood on it. When he picked me up earlier from the gym, he had no blood on his clothing.

Now anyone else would think it was from Rayvon, but that was for them to think. Like I said, I wasn't a fool. When he first left the hospital, he had this serious look on his face. Suddenly, he looked more calm, and I was more than sure it was the satisfaction of catching a body or two. Although Rayvon was okay, that wasn't enough for Truth.

As soon as we got to the car, his phone started ringing, and it was Tasha. He didn't bother to answer and that shocked me. Instead, he started the car and looked over at me.

"You hungry?" he asked, and I shook my head no.

It was too late to eat, and I was surprised he had even asked. *Yes, he's definitely out of it*, I thought, watching him as he drove in the opposite direction from my home.

"I've been looking online at apartments. I found a cute little brownstone in uptown. Do you think you can take me by there in the morning?" I asked, and he nodded *yes*.

"Why you tryna move suddenly?" he asked without looking at me.

"It's just time. I mean, I have the money. I can't live with Ms. Arnold forever."

"You right." He nodded again and got silent.

"Where are we going?" I asked to break the ice.

Since the kiss, and the way he yoked my ass up, I was happy he was being cool. Therefore, I didn't care where we were going.

Buzzzzzz...

I looked at my vibrating phone, and it was a text.

Trainer Michael: *Sorry to bother you so late. I couldn't sleep. I had a dream about your pretty ass that woke me up.*

Me: *Is that right, and what was that dream like?*

Trainer Michael: *I'd rather not say because you ain't ready.*

Me: *Is that right? And how do you know?*

Trainer Michael: *Trust me, I can tell. But when you ready, let me* *know.*

Michael blew me back by his last text. I was so smitten I didn't respond. I looked up, and I could feel Truth watching me. I didn't know why, but I was nervous and turned on. Little did Michael know, I was ready. The only reason I hadn't made a move was because I didn't know if I just wanted some dick, or did I like Michael. Whatever the case was, my pussy was beating fast every time I was around him or Truth.

When the car pulled into Truth's home, I was shocked. All the times I've been here were in the daytime, so being here this late, in the wee hours, tripped me out. Because I couldn't object. I climbed out and headed inside. When I sat down, I started texting Michael, since Truth went into his room. We were so in tune with our text Michael began to call. I answered with my bold ass, and why did I do that?

"Michael, it's late."

"I'm sorry. I just can't go back to sleep. My dick hard as fuck."

"Oh my God, you're so crazy." I burst out into a fit of laughter. "Well, I can't talk right now. I'll call you later today," I told him nervously.

I didn't give him a chance to hang up before I disconnected the line. When I looked up, Truth was standing in the doorway. I swear this nigga always popped out at the awkwardest moments. He gave me that same look he always gave me when he was mad.

I dropped my head. When I looked back up, he had his gun pointed in my direction. My head titled to the side because I didn't know what the fuck this nigga was on. I stared into his cold eyes, and my heart beat could be heard through my shirt.

Truth

With so much going on today, I couldn't believe Reign was still testing a nigga. The hood got shot up, Rayvon's little ass got hit, and now, I had to watch my ass from 12 because I made a few mothers shed tears today.

Now here it was, the one person I ran to who I considered my calm, was playing me like I was some sucka. I tried hard to lie in my bed, but the sounds of her giggles echoing through my crib set me off. She already got away with enough by texting the nigga in my car, and now this.

I lifted from my bed, and I knew after this, wasn't no turning back. Reign wanted to test my gangsta, so I was gonna give her that. I grabbed my strap from my dresser and walked right up on her. I knew I caught her off guard because her big, pretty eyes looked up at me nervously. Keep shit real, I ain't know if I would shoot or not, so I wasn't 'bout to justify wiping my strap out on her.

"Let me see yo' fucking phone," I told her as I eased closer to her. I was waiting on her to try and delete some shit because that would be my invitation to shoot her phone out her hand; and a nigga like me never missed.

When I got closer to her, I reached out with my free hand to grab it. I could see the hesitation in her face, but she knew she ain't have much of a choice. I grabbed it from her hands and went to the last caller. It only confirmed what I already knew. It was Michael. I then went to their text thread and began to read. The thread was long as hell, but I read exactly what I wanted to see. I looked back up at her and pointed my gun in her face.

"Take yo' fucking clothes off."

She looked at me, not believing I said what I said.

I bit into my lip, ready to blow her fucking weave off. I swear Reign had me twisted.

"Are you gonna rape me?" she asked, making me frown.

Where the fuck that come from? I thought to myself, looking at her like she was dumb as fuck.

"First off, I ain't gotta rape no bitch because every bitch walking this earth wanna give me some pussy. Reign, I can fuck the old white lady next door, up to the rich Black bitch with the husband, second house from the stop sign, so stop playing with me. I'm just about to give you some dick because that's what you want, right?" I asked, and she dropped her head. "Nah, don't drop yo' head. Look at me. That's what you want, right? I mean, clearly, it gotta be because you don't even know this nigga and you ready to give him some pussy. Now take yo' fucking clothes off," again, I demanded, and she stood up.

Reign slid out of her clothing, and for the first time, I saw her naked. I couldn't front, dawg. She lost a ton of weight, and her body was forming perfectly. I could tell she was embarrassed, but there was no need. A nigga been in love with Reign, and what she considered unsexy was perfect to me. Keep it real, I ain't want her thick ass to lose any more weight. However, being in the industry, it was all about looks. Therefore, I knew she wanted to keep up with the Instagram bitches.

"Truth," she called my name, knocking me out of my daze.

I stepped over to her and told her to turn around. When she did as told, I bent her over, then put my gun to the side of her head. "Reign, this pussy was mine before you gave it to me. I'll kill behind this pussy, and I'll kill you for thinking you 'bout to give it to anybody."

When she didn't reply, I sat my gun down on the table and spread her ass open so I could get a good view of her pussy. *Damn*, I thought, because it sat right there. It was pretty. It was fat, and it definitely looked tight. I slid my dick into her roughly with no remorse or condom. Whenever I wanted to let up on baby girl, I thought of the text messages I had seen. The shit made me mad as fuck, so I began to brutalize her pussy.

"Ahhhhhh, Truth! Oh my God! Truthhhhhh!" She began screaming my name.

"Nah, ma, don't call me now. You wasn't calling me when you was being a little freak bitch for that bitch nigga," I replied and continued to go in and out of her. "I'm finna put a baby in this pussy just to show you it's mine."

I dug her out. I was holding her around her neck as I fucked her from the back, and suddenly, drops of hot liquid began to fall onto my hand. I eased up a bit because her screams had turned into silent weeps. I pulled out of her and spun her around. I wasn't sure if she was crying because I was hurting her or was she scared.

"Reign, don't cry now. I'm here, and I would never hurt you."

I kissed her with so much passion. Our kiss was so intense I picked her thick ass up in one swoop and carried her to my bedroom. When we made it, I lay her down on my bed. I kissed her again, then looked her in the eyes. I couldn't help it; I put my trigger finger to her head and faked the trigger. I whispered, "I love you, and I'll kill for this pussy."

I didn't break our stare down. Tears were still pouring from her eyes, but I could tell she loosened up. With one more kiss, I fell back into my zone, only this time, I began to make love to her. I threw her legs on my shoulders and began fucking her with nice, long strokes. This time, she was moaning with light cries instead of the heavy screams she dished out at first. With every stroke, I was falling more in love. Her pussy was so damn tight I wanted to ask her if she was a virgin. The way she was talking to Michael's bitch ass told me she was experienced, but the way her pussy was feeling, I wasn't sure. Whatever the case was, Reign had the best pussy I ever fell into.

"Truth, I love you," she finally caught her breath and whispered into the air.

“I love you too, Reign Paul.” I nodded once.

I was serious. I loved Reign, and I knew after today, this was gonna be the start of something. Not only was Tasha gonna kill a nigga, but Raylen was gonna die. I really ain’t give a fuck because I was tired of Tasha’s shit, and as far as Raylen, she wasn’t my bitch. Now the scary part was when Reign found out Raylen’s baby was mine, but I would deal with that when it came. Reign wasn’t the type of chick to hide. Eventually, she would be a star, and she was gonna be my star. A nigga like me could have any bitch I wanted in the industry, but I wanted Reign Paul. Therefore, I was gonna eventually announce our relationship. Reign was worth it, and she deserved it.

Truth

Three Months Later

"And it feel like sometimes I cry
'Cause I feel so good to be alive
And there's not a doubt inside my mind
That you're still here, right here by my side..."

I watched Reign as she sang Jhene Aiko's "Summer 2020" on the Barclays Arena's stage that held at least 20,000 people. Reign had performed three songs, and so far, she kept the crowd wanting more. She had done a few songs of her own, and now, she chose this song.

I loved the beat of the song because it had that old school sample, but it was something about the lyrics that did something to me. Not to mention, the way Reign was singing it had the entire arena under her spell. As I took in the words, I smiled. She had every right to feel good and that she was alive. In the last three months, her career had taken off, and she was now headlining events. I watched Reign steadily, and the smile plastered on her face did something to me.

She was cocky as hell, and I knew it had come from all the weight she had lost, and the non-surgical lipo. Not only did her body change, but her wardrobe had done a complete 360. She dressed more sexy, and even her walk was different. I knew that had come from the way I was dicking her down and made her my bitch. One thing about me, I was a cocky ass nigga, paid, and I needed my bitch to match my fly.

Rumors of Reign and I had begun to circulate through the media and all over the world, but Reign chose to keep our shit private. Because of this, I was still able to jungle Tasha, but it was to a minimum. I really ain't give a fuck, because lately, she had been moving funny. I mean, the bitch was always moving weird, but now, it was like she was just loose.

Two weeks ago, someone sent me a picture of the bitch in the club sitting on a nigga's lap. I couldn't make out who the nigga was, but it ain't even matter. The bitch was so in her feelings over Reign she was doing shit out of spite. I really couldn't be mad because I had given Reign something I wouldn't give Tasha; love. I gave Reign a title. To the world, I was her manager with speculation, but Reign knew, like I knew, she was my bitch. Soon, the world would know. It wasn't me, it was her; but soon.

As soon as Reign stopped singing, I rushed over to the stage and escorted her off. When we made it to the back, Raylen was standing backstage. She looked at me and rolled her eyes. She then focused on Reign and began smiling. They started chit-chatting, so I went to holla at the coordinators because they wanted Reign on the next show, which was in Philly.

The entire time, I watched the two out the side of my eye, and niggas was lusting over them. Reign was a star, had lost weight, and was looking good. Since Tru, Raylen was back to herself and even kept a little thickness. Moral of the story, they were some little dimes, and niggas were hawking. I focused back on the coordinator and tried hard to speak on business until I saw a nigga who had just got off stage with Capel walk up on Reign.

I watched the nigga as he approached her with his fake ass

chain swanging. I wasn't gonna trip until Raylen began hyping the shit, and Reign smiled. I politely told the coordinator to give me a moment, and little did he know, it was a possibility his entire show was about to get turned out. I walked up on Reign, and when she saw my face, I wiped her smile right off hers.

"Let's go," I told her, and Raylen ain't have a choice but to follow.

Reign knew how I was, so she left the nigga standing there and followed with Raylen right behind. Ray knew, too, that a nigga wasn't playing. Despite her not being my bitch, she was my son's mother.

We headed out of the arena and hopped into the rented sprinter van. Because Raylen hopped in with us, I assumed she caught an Uber. I had just copped her a 2021 Range, so I didn't understand why she ain't drive herself. I slammed the door and instructed the driver to take us to the block.

I needed to get Raylen out my face and take Reign to the studio. It had been a minute since I saw my son, but I had to be discreet because when he saw me, he lit up. He was saying words, and I knew it was only a matter of time before he would say, "Dada." Reign was still in the blind, but the way Ray was acting, I could tell she was on some hater shit.

"I have to pee," Reign said, bouncing in her seat.

I told the driver to pull into the nearest gas station, because clearly, she couldn't hold it. When we pulled in, Reign jumped out fast, and Ray turned in her seat to look back at me.

"So y'all fucking now?"

"Man, don't start that shit." I shook my head and looked out the window to make sure Reign was straight.

"Whatever. I just don't understand why you gotta lie. I can tell you like her by the way you look at her. Yeah, and you almost killed that nigga at the show. I saw it all in your eyes." She kept ramping, and all I did was shake my head.

"You been knew she liked me, so why does it matter? Shit, you the one hiding shit. You sure ain't tell her that baby mine." I finally gave her the attention she wanted.

She couldn't believe I said it. Her ass got quiet and looked at me with death in her eyes. "So y'all are fucking?" she asked sadly.

"Man, Reign my bitch, Ray. You knew it was bound to happen, ma."

"And why is that? Because she lost weight and got her body done?"

"Damn, you sound like the rest of these hating hoes. Ain't that yo' best friend?" I looked at her sarcastically.

Before she could answer, Reign ran back to the van and hopped in.

"Damn, what happened that fast. Why the mad faces?" She looked between the two of us.

I remained quiet, and Ray looked at her.

"I was checking yo' man about tripping on niggas at shows. He was ready to kill that nigga," Ray remarked sarcastically.

Reign started chuckling, but she didn't catch the part about *yo' man*.

I looked at Ray like she was crazy, but I remained quiet.

"Babe, you do be trippin." Reign laughed again and didn't realize she called me babe.

"You know how I am about mine." I smirked but made sure to keep my serious face.

"But, Truth, you gotta understand niggas gon' be on me. I'm a star now, and this what comes with it." She tooted her own horn, and it made me watch her closely.

Even Ray looked at her shocked, and I could see the envy in her eyes. Reign was on her high horse, and wasn't shit wrong with it, but this was only where it started. I knew just by the remark and body language she was feeling herself, and it would only get worse.

"What the fuck!" Reign said as we all looked at the burning building.

It was Reign's old building, on fire, and it was nearly burned to a crisp. The fire department was doing their best to put out what was remaining of the fire, but it really didn't matter because the entire building was nearly gone.

Reign jumped out the van while it was slowly moving up the street and ran full speed toward the fire. I jumped out and ran behind her, leaving Ray inside the van.

"Oh my God. Apartment 5 is…is...is he okay?" Reign asked the firefighter, choked up.

"Do you know these people?" he asked, and she nodded her head yes.

"Well, I'm sorry to inform you. We have discovered a body in 4, two in 7, and one in 5. This was quite a huge fire. We haven't determined the cause yet..." He continued to talk, but the sounds of Reign's screams blocked out his voice.

I quickly pulled her into my arms and began rubbing her back. I knew exactly why she was so dismal. It wasn't about her mother, who was found in apartment 7; it was her dawg, Mr. Gary, whose body was found in 5. Over the course of time, Reign broke shit down to me about her mom and how Mr. Gary had her back. She also told me how he warned her not to fuck with me, but I couldn't blame him. A nigga sold dope, was a straight thug, and had my share with a few women. However, I was a stand up nigga when it came to my woman. It wasn't my fault Tasha wasn't shit.

Speaking of the devil, I thought because Tasha's Benz came up the street slowly, and when she saw me with my arms wrapped around Reign, she stopped so hard her car jerked. I could see her neck rolling and her mouth moving hard as she pulled alongside the curb. When Reign noticed her, she pulled back from me and frowned.

Tasha jumped out her whip and ran over to us. It was like she ain't give two fucks about the police, the fire department, or the fact that this was now a murder scene.

"This ain't the time, Tasha." I tried to wave her off so she would go.

"It's always the time. You keep telling me you don't fuck with her, but the way you just had the fat bitch wrapped in your arms looks like more than some client shit."

"Man, what the fuck I just say? She just lost her damn peoples."

"Like I said, I don't give a fuck about her or her peoples!" Tasha screamed in my face.

Before I knew it, everything happened so fast. Tasha was on the ground, and Raylen was running up the street towards us. I quickly snatched Reign up, and while I was holding her, Raylen began beating the shit out of Tasha. The girl didn't even make it off the ground. When I was finally able to snatch Ray and hold Reign back, Tasha got up crying and ran to her car.

Before she pulled off, I could see her texting on her phone. I watched her closely, and an eerie feeling came over me. She quickly sped off, and I took the girls up the street. I put Reign back into the van, and we pulled off. The moment we passed by her old building, she broke down again. It was like it all hit her at once. Damn, my heart pounded seeing her like this. I really ain't know what to do because I ain't know how to console someone.

I pulled her hand into mine, and she snatched it back hard. She looked me in the eyes, and that sorrowful look was replaced with disappointment.

I was guilty.

Reign

"We come too far to let it all end
I've told you over and over again
How I feel inside but if you go
Oh baby, there's something you should know
Something you should know,
There's something in my heart..."

Out of all the songs I've sang, this one had me so emotional. Not only did it do something to my heart, but my soul felt trapped in sorrow. It'd been a month since Mr. Gary died, along with my mother and her boyfriend. As far as them, I was numb, and no matter how much I wanted to miss my mother, I just couldn't. Now Mr. Gary, on the other hand, left me somber. Three weeks after their death, I was contacted by an insurance company. I was left with a 50 thousand dollar policy from my father. When I saw Eugene Gary in big bold letters on top of the form I liked to die. All along that man was my father and it explained why he loved me so much. When the insurance company also handed me the cause of death, I cried like a baby.

Thanks to my crackhead mother, she dozed off with a

cigarette in her hand, killing everyone. Between the agony I felt with abandoning Serenity, Mr. Gary's death only added. It wasn't a day that went by that I didn't think of Serenity. I often wondered how she looked and if she still had that same beautiful complexion. I wanted so badly to go by the address 1216, but I thought against it. I was too ashamed. Not to mention, whoever's address it was, may have turned the baby over to the authorities. I wanted so badly to tell Truth, but again, I was too embarrassed.

These days, he had so much going on I barely bothered him. I spent most of my days cooped up in my apartment while he did Lord knows. After the day I fought Tasha, I didn't trust his ass. That bitch wasn't acting like that unless he was still entertaining her. He swore she was out of the picture, but I couldn't tell. One day, I went through his phone and read a few texts. They didn't say much, but I could tell most of them were deleted. At this point, I had given up and focused on my career.

"Ladies and gentlemen, give it up for Reign!"

The sound of the audience's claps snapped me out of my daze. I looked at Lue Ella, the host of *The Midnight Show* and smiled. I walked over to the sofa and took my seat, and shortly after, Truth came from nowhere and sat next to me. Lue introduced him, and everyone clapped, already knowing who he was. Lue pulled the cue cards up after cracking a few jokes, then began asking us both questions. I tried to answer everything with honest lies that Truth and I had rehearsed.

"So Reign, Truth, can we get a little personal?" she asked, and we both laughed.

My palms got sweaty because I knew exactly what she was gonna ask. Truth and I had been asked this question a million times.

"There have been rumors sparking the air about a relationship between the two of you. Is it true?" she looked between the both of us, and I shook my head *no* as I always did.

"Yeah, that's bae." Truth chuckled, kissing me on the

cheek.

I looked at him like he was crazy.

He didn't bother looking at me as Lue threw her arms in the air to let the audience know the air was cleared. My heart began to race, and I couldn't do anything but smile to hold my composure. I was upset. Truth and I had discussed a million times that we weren't gonna put our business out into the media.

"Well, that's it for the night," Lue said after asking a few more questions.

I couldn't wait until the show was over so I could holla at Truth. I politely made my exit and headed straight to the van. Shortly after, Truth came out and climbed in. Before he took his seat, he kissed me on the cheek and sat down.

I spun around in my chair and looked at him. "What was that back there, Truth?"

"What?"

"Truth, you know what. You really told them people we were together."

"So what?" He shrugged his shoulders.

"The fuck you mean, 'so what'? Truth, we agreed to keep shit between us."

"Reign, you my bitch! Who the fuck I got to hide from!"

"Shit, the media like we agreed!" I matched his energy and stood to my feet. "I don't want my business out there. Truth, I love you, but we have to keep it professional."

He sat quietly momentarily, and I could see the shock all over his face.

"So how about we just don't fuck around?" He then jumped to his feet and mugged me.

My face frowned because I couldn't believe what he was saying. Before I could reply, my phone began to ring, and it was Oshey. I damn near ain't wanna answer, but I had to because we were meeting her at the next location.

Oshey was, I guess, my new friend. She did PR work for

me, compliments of Truth. She was actually cool, and over the course of six months, I actually took a liking to her. Hell, she knew everything about my entire life, and even my personal business. I opened up to her about Truth and I's relationship, and even Mr. Gary's passing. One thing I would never do was mention the baby to anyone. That was going to the grave with me. However, I told her everything that had to do with my love life. She said she suspected Truth and me were an item, but she wasn't gonna ask. Little did she know, had she asked, Truth would have definitely confirmed.

"Hello?"

"Damn, why you sound so dry? Where are you guys?"

"Ugh, girl, nothing. We on our way now. We're about eighteen minutes away." I looked down at my GPS.

"Okay, well, I'm here. I'mma head to our section and wait on you guys."

"Okay," I replied and disconnected.

I focused my attention out the window because I was still in my feelings. Anything not to look at Truth.

"I don't know why you're tripping? Y'all are together, Reign. A committed relationship at that. I can't say I don't blame him for acting like that." Oshey nodded her head towards Truth.

He was standing by the VIP exit with a cup in his hand and a chick in front of him. I swear it took everything in me not to knock his ass in the back of the head with my Hennessy bottle.

Oshey wasn't making shit any better.

"I can blame him. Shit, we agreed to keep it between us." I rolled my eyes and looked in Truth's direction.

He was really entertaining this bitch right in my face. I watched them both with so much hatred in my heart I didn't even hear the young lady who stood beside me asking for a picture. I was so in my feelings I wanted to say no, but I wasn't that type. I stood up for the picture, and it took everything in me to muster up the biggest fake smile. Once the picture was done, I sat back down and threw back another shot. Tonight, I was good and drunk, and it seemed like the drunker I got, the more I wanted to fight.

"I swear I wanna fight." I looked at Oshey.

"You need something to calm you down," she said and went into her bag. I couldn't see what she pulled out, but moments later, she had it on a small, metal object. "Here. Just sniff it. Long and hard friend."

"Is this coke?" I asked, taking the small object from her.

"Everybody in here gets down. Trust me, you'll feel so much better."

I looked around the club timidly, and everyone was so in tune with one another, nobody noticed what was going on. I took the object to my nose, and as quick as I scanned the room, I quickly took it all up my nose. For a moment, I had a slight burn, then suddenly, I felt better. I sat back in my seat and let the effects of the coke kick in. Oshey was right. I wasn't tripping off Truth any longer, however, my body did grow hot. For some reason, I wanted to fuck, and, of course, it was gonna be Truth. I waited for him to finish doing him so we could leave.

In the meantime, I threw back shot after shot, and I never noticed how drunk I was until I stood to my feet. I wanted so badly to kick my heels off in the club, but I just couldn't. When I felt Oshey grab my hand, I felt secure, and we made our way to the van. I guess she was on the same thing I was on; we both were ready to go.

Oshey ended up staying with me until Truth finally decided to bring his ass out. When he climbed into the van, I was already waiting on him with my dress up and pussy out. He stopped and looked at me strangely, but what was so strange about me wanting to fuck? I mean, my pussy was sitting out for him to attack it. I didn't know if it was the coke or liquor, but I swear I was feeling myself. I had gained a certain urge of encouragement, and I could tell that was exactly what Truth was thinking.

However, he walked over to where I lay, and his eyes hungrily watched my pussy. I began fingering myself, and clearly, this shit turned him on more because he walked over to me and began helping.

"Ohhhh, shitt!" I moaned loudly, not giving a fuck about Ford, our Caucasian driver. "Stick it in, Truth, pleeeease," I begged, growing tired of him fingering my pussy.

He stepped out his shoes, followed by his clothing, and I continued to masturbate because I was horny as hell. The moment he was done, he took my legs into the cuff of his arms and spread them far apart. He slid his dick inside of me, and I instantly began panting. I'd be a damn lie if I said Truth wasn't the muthafucking truth. He had that dope dick that I begged for daily. After the first day we fucked, I had become addicted to his sexual pleasures, and if he thought he was gonna take that from me, he was a fool. I craved this shit, and it was definitely because of his stroke game and size. His dick was huge, and his strokes were always on time. It had only been about ten minutes, and already, I was about to cum.

"Ahhhhhhhhhh!" I screamed out as I felt my juices flowing.

He continued to fuck me roughly, and normally, I would surrender. Not now. I swear the coke had me feeling like Superwoman, and I wanted all the smoke. Truth must have sensed it because from time to time, he looked at me puzzled.

I took it upon myself to lift up and bend my ass over the leather seat. He knew this was how I liked it, so he granted me the time I needed to prepare myself and spread my own ass. He slid himself into me and began ramming in and out of me with aggression.

"Shitttttt...Daddyyyy....yassss...fuck this pussy, Truth! Fuck me harder, nigga!" And he did just that. I began gasping, barely able to breathe. It felt like his dick was hitting ligaments I didn't know could be reached. "Gotttttt damnnnnn! I love youuuuuu! Shittt, I love this dick!"

It seemed like the more I screamed, the more he performed. I could feel his dick growing bigger, and I knew from fucking him constantly this meant he was on the verge of cumming. I began matching his strokes and throwing my ass back, making sure it slammed into him hard. Suddenly, a gush of hot cum began to fill my pussy up, and it made me cum right along with him. My body began to shake, and the urge of peeing came, letting me know I was about to squirt. This was something Truth taught me, and sometimes, I couldn't control it. It flew out my pussy, causing a complete mess.

I knew it was all over the both of us, and I was sure it had fucked up the van. When he pulled out of me, I stayed in the doggy style position, trying hard to regroup. When I found my momentum, I flipped over and continued to finger myself. That coke had definitely did a number on me because I was still hot and bothered and wanted him to fuck me more. Truth stood back and watched because this was a side of me he'd never seen. Hell, it was a side of myself I'd never seen.

"I love you." I moaned, looking him in the eyes.

Instead of him replying, he headed to the back of the van and lay down. No, "I love you" back, so I knew now he was still upset. *He'll get over it*, I thought as I continued to bring myself to another nut.

Reign

"What's up, Reign?"

I turned around because I heard my name being called. I mean, it was typical now that my status had begun to grow. However, it was something about the way he said it that told me he knew me personally. I spun on my heels and came face to face with Devin. My face instantly frowned while he still held a smile. He walked over and reached out to give me a hug, but I pulled back.

"Nah, nigga. Ain't none of that."

"Damn." He chuckled and tilted his head to one side. "What I do?"

"You know what you did. Got my best friend over there with that damn baby, and yo' ass won't step up to the plate. That's fucked up, Devin."

"Wait, what?" He got choked up, and again, he titled his head. "Fuck you talking 'bout, ma?"

"I'm talking 'bout Tru. You know, your baby by Raylen you said fuck it about."

"Raylen? Baby?" His face frowned, and I swear he looked

lost. "Reign, I got one daughter, and she's nine."

"So you don't know about this baby, or you feel the baby ain't yours?" I asked because this man stood here as if he ain't no shit about Tru.

"How old is this baby?"

"He's almost one."

"Nah, hell nah. I ain't fucked Raylen in three years. I ran into her a couple months back, but she ain't give me any play. Shit, she fucking with that nigga, Truth."

"Nah, that's all me, but okay, Devin. My bad." I had to apologize.

I headed to my car, and when I sat down in my seat, I began thinking about Raylen and why she lied. She told me all types of stories of talking to Devin, having run-ins with him, and how he even said he would step up to the plate to be the father. Now here it was, this man had no knowledge of a baby. I mean, it was her business, but why lie? Why lie to me? I was the last person who could judge any situation. Hell, she knew how I grew up, and if she knew the skeletons I kept hidden, maybe she'd keep shit real. Whatever the case was, I wanted to confront her, so I jumped in my car and headed for the hood. I had a three p.m. hair appointment, and because it was only one p.m., I knew I had time. I just had to know.

When I pulled up on Ray's street, there was a big commotion, and the streets were filled with people. It looked like a bit much going on, but when I saw Tasha standing on her car shouting, and Ray being held back by her brother, I quickly pulled over and jumped out. I ran over to where Ray stood to let her know I was ready to throw down. Tasha had two chicks with her, but I knew with Rayvon right here, and these hood niggas, they wouldn't dare let shit happen to her.

"Yeah, tell her!" Tasha shouted, looking at Raylen.

I looked at Ray, and her reaction was pale.

Tasha kept screaming, "Tell her!" and curiosity got the best of me.

I focused on Ray with anticipation, and whatever it was, I could tell she wasn't gonna say shit. I looked back at Tasha, and she nodded her head.

"Yeah, bitch ain't tell you that baby belongs to Truth!" Tasha pursed her lips tauntingly, then looked back at Raylen.

Raylen's eyes grew wide when she looked at me. The way she looked made what Tasha said begin to register. I knew I heard her right. The baby was Truth's, and the sound of those words knocked the wind out of me.

"Is this true, Ray?" I asked, finally able to speak.

She didn't reply, but her eyes began to well with tears.

"Hell yeah, it's true. I went through that nigga phone," Tasha said and pulled her phone out to show me. She held it out as if I would take it, but I didn't need her receipts; the proof was in the pudding.

I shook my head, unable to believe it, but it was true. Tears began to fall from my eyes as I backed away from her slowly. I was out of it. I never paid attention to Rayvon screaming down her throat. The way he looked told me he ain't know either. I climbed into my car, and my hands shook so hard I could barely grip the steering wheel. Tears fell rapidly, and all I wanted to do was kill Truth's ass. Granted, Raylen played a big part in all this, but Truth was the one who laid down and slept with me. I was gonna holla at her later.

Ring...Ring...Ring...

I opened my eyes because my phone wouldn't stop ringing.

"Hello?"

"Reign! Where the hell are you? I've been calling you, Truth been calling you, even Melvin said he's been calling you for makeup."

Oh, shit, I thought, looking at the top of the phone for the time. I had a photoshoot for the *Freshman XXL* magazine edition. I looked at the plate that sat next to me and thought of the many lines of coke I had sniffed before passing out. This explained my headache and why I slept so hard.

"I'm not gonna make it," I told Oshey, knowing she was gonna question me.

"What do you mean, you not going?"

"I'm just not in the mood. Tell them use an old picture." I hung up the phone.

Moments later, Truth called, but I didn't bother answering. The nigga had his nerves because I called him all night, and he ain't bother answering. Therefore, I powered off my phone and closed my eyes so I could get some rest. However, that ain't work.

I opened my eyes to the sound of pounding on my front door, and I knew it was only Truth. I tried hard to ignore it, but he wouldn't go away, so it only forced me to get up. I lifted from the bed and took the plate into the kitchen. I made sure to check the mirror so there was no coke residue on my nose. I made my way to the door, and when I opened it, he stood there watching me with so much regret in his eyes. I really ain't know if I wanted to stab him, fight him, or shoot his dumb ass, so I burst out into tears. I didn't know what else to do. I was hurt.

"Reign!" He quickly grabbed me before I fell to the ground. He pulled me inside and closed the door behind us. I was sobbing so hard he had no choice but to lie my body down on the ground. He bent down over me and looked me in my eyes. "Reign, I swear it ain't what it looks like. I fucked that girl twice, and she got pregnant. You weren't my bitch then, ma, so you can't really be mad," he had the nerve to say.

I nodded my head *yes* and reached out for him to help me off the ground. Tears still poured from my eyes, but he was right. "You're right, Truth." I was finally able to speak as I eased my way over to the coffee table.

Before he knew it, I picked up the lamp and swung it so hard it crashed into the wall. It missed his dumb ass by an inch. When he came up, he looked at me unbelievably, but I wasn't done. I rushed his ass and began swinging nonstop. I got about six licks in before he crashed both our bodies into the ground. He held my hands over my head and tried hard to reason.

"I'm sorry, ma," he spoke so genuinely, but I wasn't falling for that shit.

"You and that bitch been in my fucking face this whole time! Nigga, you even gave me a ride to the hospital!" I tried to swing again, but he caught my hands and pinned them above me again. "This whole time, y'all been in my face!" I burst out into a new set of tears. "I understand I wasn't yo' bitch, nigga, but y'all hid that shit after I became yours! Ugh, I'm so done with you and that hoe! She knew I was in love with you! She knew how I felt about you since we were kids, Truth! Why did she get to have you? Because I was the dirty little girl from down the street! Huh!"

"Reign, chill, please."

"Nah, keep it real! Was it!"

"You always been pretty to me. I don't know, man. It was the night of her birthday. Shit happened," he spoke as I watched his full lips move.

Truth was so damn fine, but right now, he was ugly to me. After losing Mr. Gary, I thought that no pain could amount to that pain I was feeling, but I was wrong. The more he talked, the more I hated him. He was trying so hard to look sincere, but it wasn't working. The nigga even had the nerve to bend down and kiss me. I accepted his kiss, but that electrifying feeling just wasn't there. I didn't know if I'd ever get over this, but right now, I wasn't fucking with Truth. I was gonna do me in the industry and elevate in my career without this nigga. As bad as it would hurt to let him go, I had to. I loved Truth more than life itself, but I couldn't bear looking at him knowing my damn God son was his child. That was a slap in the face, and it stung. I was cool on dude, and no matter how much of a sob story he gave me, I ignored that shit.

Truth

After I left Reign's crib, I hoped in my whip, feeling like shit. I expected after hitting her off with this dope dick I'd square things away with her, but that shit ain't work. I could tell by her body language and nonchalant attitude she wasn't fucking with me. I knew it was a matter of time this shit would hit the fan, and thanks to Tasha's stupid ass, it did just that.

Last night, I let the dumb bitch come over so I could fuck, and the moment I went to sleep, she start going through my phone. There were messages between Raylen and I discussing Tru. Of course, I referend to him as my son, so it was a dead bang giveaway. I only fucked with Tasha because I was still in my feelings about the *Ella Show*. Reign had a nigga fucked up. I understood we were supposed to keep shit private, but I couldn't. She belonged to me, and I wanted the world to know. It was crazy because that was what every woman in the world wanted. They wanted a nigga to rep them, whether it was on social media or walking in public. Nah, that wasn't the case for Reign. The shit had me hot, because there were bitches dying to be in her shoes, but I chose her.

"Yeah?" I answered my phone for Rayvon, already knowing what the nigga wanted. Nigga had called my phone a few times, but I wasn't prepared to talk.

"So that's how we moving now?"

"Man, look. I ain't gotta answer to no nigga. Raylen grown, dog."

"Damn, Truth, you supposed to be my mans. But since you wanna act high power like what you did is right, keep that same energy!" nigga shouted through the phone.

I swear I couldn't bust my U fast enough. He disconnected the phone, and I did 100 miles an hour, all the way to the hood. I wanted that nigga to keep the same energy.

When I pulled up, his Maserati was parked out front, and the door was wide open to their crib. As soon as I jumped out, he was coming out of the house. The look on my face must have alerted him, because his face frowned, and he matched my aggression. I guess at this point, there was nothing to be said.

We met each other halfway and began locking up instantly. We went blow for blow until I got tired of playing with the nigga. I picked him up off his feet and slammed him right on his head. Ms. Arnold must have heard the commotion because she ran outside and began shouting for us to stop.

"Ma, this bitch had a baby by this nigga!" he shouted, looking from Raylen to me.

Ms. Arnold was puzzled as she looked between the three

of us. She then looked down at Tru, who was snuggled close in Raylen's arms. "Is this true, Raylen?" she asked, and Raylen nodded her head *yes*.

"I swear y'all two bitches!" Rayvon started raging.

"You betta watch yo' mouth." I glared at the nigga. I ain't give a fuck if his moms was right here.

"Rayvon, well, your sister is grown," she tried to reason so she could calm Rayvon down.

"Grown? *Grown*? What the fuck that mean? They supposed to be sister and brother! This was my nigga!" He threw another bitch fit and stormed up the street.

I looked over at Ms. Arnold, and to my surprise, she ain't look too pissed. I bent down and kissed Tru's cheek because I had too much shit to do. I made a 'bout face to my whip and climbed in. I headed straight for Tasha's crib, hoping like hell she would be there. Because this bitch was to blame for all this. I was about to put my foot so far up her ass she would taste my sole.

Because I had Tasha ducked off in a loft in Jersey, it took me forty minutes to get to her crib. Instead of the normal underground parking, I pulled up in the front because I was only gonna be here for a few minutes. I headed into the building and took the elevator up. When I made it to the twelfth floor, I pulled my keys from my pocket and headed for the door.

I could hear music playing from on the other side of the door. I stuck my key inside and headed in. I stormed down the hall for Tasha's bedroom, and when I got near the door, the sound of her voice blazed through the air. She was screaming at the top of her lungs as if she were dying. But nah, I knew better.

Tasha was getting her back blown out. I knew that scream from anywhere.

A part of me wanted to just leave and let her do her, but fuck that. I stepped further into the room, and they never even looked up. I pulled my strap from my waist and used the butt to tap the back of ol boy's head. He quickly turned around, and Tasha instantly jumped up. I looked from the nigga to Tasha in disbelief. I was already upset from the shit with Rayvon, and now, my blood had just reached its limit.

"Truth!" Tasha said my name, trying to stall me, but it was too late.

I fired six shots into Cugo's body, making him crash into the wall. When I knew he was dead, I looked at Tasha, and she wore this frantic look. I swear it took everything in me not to blow the bitch's brains out. Instead, I hopped onto the bed and began assaulting her with my strap.

Wam! Wam! Wam! Wam! Wam! Wam! Wam! Wam! Wam! Wam! Wam! Wam! Wam! Wam! Wam!

I hit her repeatedly with my gun until both her eyes were shut, and she blanked out. As my chest heaved up and down, I looked over to my arch enemy, not fucking believing that Tasha would stoop so low. This wasn't just an enemy; this was the nigga who had been terrorizing the hood. Our war's been going since the '90s, so this bitch couldn't act like she ain't know. This nigga Cugo had his whole hood behind him, and just like in my hood, he was that nigga. The nigga who ran them niggas, got all the money, and put fear in them.

I looked at Tasha one last time, then made my way out the door. The entire way to my car, I thought about how long had she been fucking with him. Knowing Tasha, she *been* sneaking around with this nigga. Now that I thought about it, she prolly was the one telling this nigga every time I was on the block. I could remember times the bitch would ask where I was at, and the block would get shot up. That shit was making perfectly good sense. I shook my head, not believing this bitch. I wanted so bad to kill her, but I let her live because I was gonna torture that hoe by making her life hell.

Tasha knew the type of nigga I was, and she still tested me. Therefore, she was gonna have to pay one way or the other. I needed to get Reign back in my good graces so we could move on for good. Now that Tasha was out of the picture, I could focus on my relationship. This was the move I needed and wasn't no looking back for Tasha. It was only up from here, but like I said, this bitch was gonna suffer.

Reign

Several Months Later

"Why are you here?"

"The fuck you mean, why I'm here? Reign, stop playing with me."

"I'm serious. Just leave. I don't need you here. I don't need a babysitter, Truth."

"Man, since when am I a babysitter? All this shit ain't possible without me."

"Nigga, I'm the one with the voice. You ain't did shit for my fucking career." I rolled my eyes and dismissed him.

I was trying to finish partying, and with Truth here, I couldn't sniff my coke and flirt with the guys.

From the side of my eyes, I could see him still standing there. I walked away fast so he would get the picture. I wasn't fucking with Truth, and I meant it. His ass was only here to pacify me, and like I said, I ain't need a damn sitter. Really, I ain't need his services any longer. He'd made enough money off me, so he could get the fuck on.

"Reign, you want yours?" this white boy named Kenny yelled out, referring to a line of coke.

I looked back to see if Truth was still here, and he was. "Not right now, Ken. My fake daddy is here," I replied and took a seat next to his girlfriend, Tiffany.

Just as I picked up my cup, my phone rang. When I saw it was Raylen, I rolled my eyes in shock. I wanted so badly to ignore her, but I was curious as to why she was calling.

"Hellooo?"

"Reign?" she called my name as if she knew I was surprised I answered.

"Yeah, what's up?"

"I just wanted to tell you I'm sorry. Reign, your my best friend, and I knew how in love you were with him. It only happened a couple times. To be honest, I never thought you guys would be together. You were always so shy and ummmm...ummmm..." She began pausing.

"What? I was too fat? I was a slop?"

"No...well, yes. I knew the type of women Truth liked, so I never thought he would be with you. I'm sorry," she apologized sadly.

I kinda understood where she was coming from because it was all true. However, that didn't justify that sneaking and geeking.

"Look, I understand, but y'all could have told me. Raylen, had I known, I wouldn't have fallen in love with him."

"I know."

"Well, you can have him. I'm good on the nigga now." I looked up just in time to see him walk away.

"Nah, I'm a good friend. That man is in love with you. Anyway, I wanted to invite you to Tru's birthday party. It's here at the house. Nothing much, just ice cream and cake. Please come. He misses you."

"I'll see if I'm free. What day is it?"

"It's tomorrow, but we're gonna have a bigger party the following Saturday."

"A'ight. I will if I can."

"Okay. Well, I can hear you're busy. Again, I'm sorry."

"Okay," I replied and hung up the phone.

Now that Truth was gone, I was able to dive back into some coke and relax. I called out to Kenny and let him know I was ready. He hit me off with four lines, and I followed up with a nice swallow of Rum. Truth had fucked up my high, but I was almost back. I lay my head back and let the drugs take effect. For a brief moment, I thought of Raylen and I's call until I was numb and nothing bothered me. Not Raylen, not Truth, and definitely not the fans who continuously wanted pictures.

The next morning, I woke up feeling like shit. I had the worst hangover, but nothing that a little coke couldn't fix. After taking a few lines, I found my willpower to get dressed. Once I was done, I headed out the door. I decided to pull up to Tru's cake and ice cream. I didn't plan on staying long, so I was gonna give him some money and go. I really ain't wanna be bothered with Raylen, and I damn sure didn't wanna be bothered with Truth. This was his son, so I knew he was gonna be there.

When I pulled up to the block, I looked over at my old building and thought of Mr. Gary. I quickly turned my head so I didn't get emotional, but I did notice the building had been nicely remodeled. I kept going and pulled up to Raylen's. I parked behind a police patrol car, wondering why they were here. I also noticed Truth's Lamborghini parked across the street, so I knew I really wasn't gonna stay long. I climbed out of the car and headed to the door. It was slightly ajar, so I opened it. There were two cops standing in the living room, along with a child, and because they were introducing themselves, I knew they had just arrived.

"Rayvon Arnold?" one of the cops asked, looking dead at Rayvon. The scared look on his face must have told the police he was nervous because they quickly informed him he wasn't under arrest. "We wanted to speak to you about this child, Serenity Paul. Because of your arrest record, we were able to match a DNA sample with yours, and the child is yours. The parents who had custody of the child passed away, so we thought we'd give you a chance to get custody before she was put up for adoption."

Hearing Serenity's name made me look down and get a good look at my daughter. The first thing I noticed was the raindrop birth mark on the side of her eye, and I knew this was my baby. My eyes bucked, and everyone standing in the room looked shocked.

"A baby?" Miesha looked at him, then to the cops.

Both cops looked at one another, knowing they had just started some shit. One of them cleared his throat nervously, and I swear I felt that shit because I swallowed hard too.

"So will you be willing?" the officer asked, but Rayvon didn't reply.

"Paul?" Raylen mumbled, looking at me.

Of course, she knew my last name, so I could see the curiosity in her eyes.

"I ain't got no fucking baby," Rayvon finally spoke up, jumping to his feet.

The cops looked at one another, and one sighed, frustrated. He knew Rayvon was the daddy, and it agitated him that he wouldn't step up. At this point, I ain't know what to do. Truth hadn't caught on, but the guilt inside of me told me I had to own up to my child. I swallowed another lump in my throat, then found my will power to speak up.

"She's my child," I spoke in a low tone, but enough for everyone to hear me.

The entire room gasped, and it made me drop my head embarrassed.

"Reign Paul?" one of the officers asked, and I nodded my head *yes*.

"Would you like to have your child back?" he asked, and again, I nodded my head.

I looked at Truth, and I could see the hurt and anger all over his face. When he stormed out of the room, the front door slammed so hard everyone jumped.

"Rayvon, is this true?" Ms. Arnold asked.

"Hell nah. I ain't got no baby, and definitely not by *her*," he lied, referring to me as *her*. His ass couldn't hit me with a fat joke any longer, so now I was just *her*.

I rolled my eyes as the officers handed me a card for where to go. I took the card and bent down to Serenity. I brushed a strand of her wild, curly hair from her face and rubbed her little chin.

"Mommy's gonna come get you, baby," I told her as tears began to slide down my face. I stood to my feet and looked at Rayvon. "Nigga, you know this yo' baby. Keep playing with me, and I'll tell everyone in this room how this baby was made, you little bitch." I furiously looked at him, ready to fight his ass.

I swear one slick thing out his mouth I was gonna beat the fuck out of him and his bitch.

Miesha jumped to her feet and stormed out just as Truth had done. I ain't give a fuck. Fuck all these people. I walked out and jumped into my car. I sat here for a moment contemplating my next move. I was going to get my baby, but I wasn't sure if I would get tested. I couldn't take the chance of them finding coke in my system. At this point, I really didn't know what to do. I couldn't leave Serenity hanging again, so I had to think quickly. But first, I was gonna find Truth and plead my case. I needed him to understand it wasn't as he thought. I knew he was tripping, because here I was, tripping over him and Raylen when all along I had my own skeletons. I could only imagine what he was thinking, and I prayed like hell he would have some understanding.

After discovering Truth wasn't at home, I pulled up to the studio where I was hoping he would be. As soon as I spotted his car, I quickly parked and climbed out. I still had a pool of tears in my eyes, and imagining Truth's face when he stormed out only hurt more. The pain I was feeling now was unbearable. Not even the coke was helping. I pulled over several times to take a sniff, but I wasn't getting that same effect.

After taking a long, hard sigh, I stepped out of the car and made my way into the old Cabana. Truth had kept the club and now named it The Purple Cabana. I headed through the door and went upstairs to the studio. When I walked in, Truth was sitting behind the soundboard with a bottle of Remy Martin in his hands. He didn't bother to turn around, but his voice erupted through the room.

"Just leave me alone, Reign," he spoke, feeling my presence.

"I need to talk to you."

"Ain't shit to talk about."

"Truth, please," I cried out and closed the door behind me. "You don't have to talk, just listen." I paused, waiting for him to say some slick shit, but he didn't. "I'm so sorry. I know things seem crazy, and they are. Truth, you have to understand that none of this was to hurt you."

"Huhhh," he mumbled sarcastically.

"I swear, Truth. You or no one else will ever understand."

"Understand? *Understand*? How the fuck could I understand you having a whole muthafucking baby by a nigga who calls himself my brother? The real trip part is, you tried to trip on me for having a baby and not telling you, but you did the same shit." He shook his head. "Just get the fuck away from me and far before I hurt you. In my eyes, you're a dead bitch."

Damn, I thought, and I felt like a dagger had pierced me right through the heart. I knew he meant what he said, so I turned to walk away defeated. Before I walked out the door, I looked back at him. "That man raped me. He took my virginity and against my will. He told me if I told anyone, he would kill me. Truth, I left that baby on a stranger's step too ashamed. That alone took a chunk of my heart. Now, the last bit of heart I have left you just took. I'll leave you alone for good."

I walked out of the room with a heavy heart. My heart was aching, and I felt dizzy. My emotions were running wild because I never meant for any of this to happen. At this point, I felt like I wanted to die. I had that same feeling I had as a child when I suffered abuse from my mother. Truth was the only person I felt cared genuinely about me, and now, I had no one. As I pulled off from the Cabana, I felt alone and abandoned. All I wanted to do was go hide under a rock and just fucking die.

Truth

Six Months Later..

"You gotta see this."

I looked up, and Tony was walking through the door. He held a newspaper in his hand and dropped it on my desk. I picked up the paper and began reading the headline.

Pop Star, Reign Paul, Drug Addiction. As I began reading, I looked up at Tony every chance I could. I shook my head, and to see this had a nigga's heart hurting. No matter where Reign and I were, I still had a soft spot for little mama. Every time I looked up, she was in the blogs either fighting or just doing some weird shit. After the day she told me I didn't do shit for her career, that was the day I stepped away to let her run her own program.

Never in a million years I would think she would get addicted to drugs and be out here wildin' out. Her eyes were always glossy, and she was losing herself in the industry. The fame had taken Reign under, and it was beginning to show. Over the last six months, it was like her whole world was crumbling. She never got custody of her daughter because she tested positive for cocaine. Raylen ended up getting her because Rayvon didn't want shit to do with the child.

I did whatever I could to help Raylen take care of Serenity because I felt she was a part of me. Every time I looked at that little girl, I thought of Reign because she was the spitting image of her. To know Serenity was a product child of rape made me wanna protect her from the world. For months, I thought of killing that nigga, Rayvon, and the only thing that saved the nigga was Raylen. I knew it would hurt her and Ms. Arnold, so I spared the nigga's life.

However, I cut him off and left the nigga out here dry. Miesha had finally left his ass for good and ran off with a local D Boy. Rayvon's weird ass was shacked up with Porsha up the street, and if I didn't know any better, I'd think the nigga was on drugs. He was looking bad out here. I knew it was only a matter of time before his karma would catch up with his ass and that time was now.

"She has a show tonight for BET. Biggest show of her career, Truth. I don't think she should do it," Tony said, bringing me from my daze.

I looked at him, and I could see the hurt in his eyes. Tony loved the fuck outta Reign, and because of her, I still kept him around. I let him run the Cabana, and he was making more money than he ever did. I also used him as a scout, and he was bringing me more talent. I had a total of three artists, and their careers were taking off. However, none of them could fill Reign's shoes.

"Ain't shit we can do. Reign is grown, and she knows what she is doing," I replied dismissively.

He stared out into the air like he was in a daze, but there was nothing we could do. He walked out of my office, and I got up to leave.

As I drove down highway 86, Reign was on my mind heavy. A part of me wanted to go to her show, but because of her constant rejection, I chose not to. I hadn't seen her in a little over six months, but I watched her from afar. Raylen had spoken to her a couple times, so she knew Serenity was in her care, but she still didn't put in any effort to see her.

I couldn't believe after years of seeing her mother under the spell of drugs, she would resort to drugs. Whether it was rocked up or in powder form, the drug was a drug, and it had taken many lives. The shit was so sad it made me wanna stop selling it.

When I pulled up to my crib, I headed inside and straight for the shower. I was gonna call it a night because I had a busy day ahead of me tomorrow. It was only 9:56 p.m., which was early for me, but I was drained. Right now, a nigga couldn't think straight. Reign had my head all fucked up, but like I said, it wasn't shit I could do for her.

After taking my shower, I went to sit inside my den so I could take a few shots and watch some TV until I dozed off. I grabbed a bottle and nestled up on my sofa with the remote. I went to BET because they were showing the concert live. It featured MoneyBagg Yo, Meg, H.E.R., and Reign Paul. I began watching, and Megan Thee Stallion had just finished performing. I watched a couple more acts until they announced Reign, who was the last performer.

The beat to her song "Summer Love" came on, and this

was the song that made her career blossom. She strutted onto the stage followed by six dancers. She was looking good as hell, but I could see the exhaustion in her face. She had lost more weight, and I knew it was because of the drugs, and not from her working out.

For a moment, she had the crowd rocking until her voice began to crack. On camera, you could see people getting up from their seats, and I even heard a few people booing her. She tried hard to finish her song until she noticed she wasn't getting the normal reaction from the crowd. Suddenly, her voice cracking began echoing through the mic, and I assumed they shut the mic off in the middle of her performance. When her body crashed into the ground, I jumped to my feet. My phone began ringing nonstop, but I was so in tune with the TV I ignored it.

I continued to watch, and Reign had a pool of tears pouring from her eyes. It was like she had a mental breakdown right on stage. Seeing Reign cry like that did something to me and the shit made me shed a tear. I heard my phone ring again, and it brought me to. However, I didn't bother answering. Instead, I ran upstairs at full speed and slid into my clothing.

I then flew out the door and headed for the show. I did 100 miles an hour all the way there and made it in no time. I knew they wouldn't give me any problems with getting in because I was now a big name in the industry. I was not only a manager because I did more producing. I produced a few tracks for all kinds of rappers and singers.

When I made it backstage, I began browsing the rooms for Reign. The stampede of cameramen let me know exactly where she was. It was hard, but I got through the crowd and was finally able to find her. She was swarmed with cameras, and I could see the frustration all over her face. It was like nobody was helping her, not even the arena's security. I bogarded my way inside, knocking over whoever was in my way. I ran over to her side, and she was still crying. She looked up at me with the most pitiful set of eyes, and our eyes locked.

"Truth…" She called my name, not believing it was me.

Just seeing me made her begin to cry harder, but right now, we couldn't have that fairytale moment. I swooped her into my arms and carried her out of the arena. She held onto me tightly and buried her face into my chest. When we made it to the car, I tossed her in and ran over to the driver side so we could get the hell out of dodge. Before I pulled off, she looked over at me and finally smiled.

"Thank you," she spoke lowly.

I nodded my head without any words. Reign was my muthafucking dawg, so there was no need to thank me. I had her back, and at this point, I was gonna get her the help she needed because I needed her to bounce back. This wasn't the same girl I had fallen in love with, and I needed her back. I was gonna do anything I could to get Reign back, and I was gonna die trying.

Reign

One Year Later

"Ms. Paul, you have a visitor."

"Okay. Thank you, Diane."

"You're welcome, honey. Run along, don't keep him waiting." She closed the door behind her and headed out.

I didn't know why, but I was a nervous wreck. I was actually like this every time Truth showed up to the facility. I was still slightly embarrassed by everything that had happened, and although an entire year had passed by, I couldn't shake the feeling.

I stood up from the bed and made my way out the door. When I walked into the main room, Truth was seated just as he had done for the entire year. When he noticed me, he smiled blissfully, and it made me blush. Our eyes connected, and we held each other's gaze for a spare moment and that only melted me more. For the entire year, I spent the days recovering inside of the Women's Recovery Facility, and Truth was right by my side.

It had been a year since I've been clean, and my body needed it. I didn't know where, and I didn't know how, but somewhere along the lines, I completely lost myself in the industry. What I thought was helping me fight battles was actually a demon in disguise. The drug made me hurt people I loved and that same abandonment I had endured from my mother I did to my own child. Thanks to Raylen, she had gotten full custody of Serenity, and I owed her my life.

"Bring yo' sexy ass here," Truth said, making me blush harder.

I ran over to him, and he wrapped his arms around me, then kissed me on the forehead. Every time he called me sexy it, did something to me. Since I've been in this facility, I picked up a little weight, and he swore he loved it.

"Thank you for coming, Truth."

"No need for thanks, ma. You know I got you." He smiled and rubbed my chin. "Let's get up outta here today. I cleared yo' pass with the director already."

"Umm, okay," I agreed, looking down at my clothing.

"You look good, baby girl. Stop tripping."

He grabbed my hand and led me out of the facility. When we got outside, I already knew the brand new Aston Martin was his, and it was beautiful. He opened my door to let me inside, and I fell into the comfy leather seats. He ran around to the other side and climbed in. He hit the Bluetooth for the radio, and a girl began to sing lovingly through the speakers.

"Who's that?" I asked because she sounded good.

"That's my artist, Vetta Kayne. She dope, huh?"

"Yeah, she is," I replied a little jealous, but I couldn't front; she was.

"Don't look like that, ma. Can't nobody fade you. You got an angelic ass voice that melts a nigga."

I was so busy smiling I couldn't even reply.

"So how you feeling, ma?"

"I'm great."

"You ready to get back to it?"

"Ummm, I don't know, Truth. You saw how the crowd did me last time."

"Yeah, that was a year ago. Trust me, the world is ready for you."

I sat back in my seat and gave what he was saying some thought. One thing I always did was trust Truth. He believed in me when no one else did.

"You know they found Tasha dead?" Truth asked more so telling me because I didn't know. I turned in my seat to look at him in total disbelief. He was nodding his head yes as he gripped the steering wheel. Before I could ask, he was already confirming the cause of death was suicide. The way Truth looked when he said it, told me something was fishy about it but like I always said, it wasn't my damn business. I hated to hear something like this but just like Rayvon, it was Tasha's Karma. Rayvon had ended up on drugs and the little bitch never wanted to take responsibility of my daughter but it was cool because Raylen, Truth and Ms. Arnold did a great damn job.

Epilogue

"Ladies and gentlemen, we have a surprise guest. She's been gone for a moment, but she's back, live, right here on our stage. Everyone, give a warm welcome to a true star, Reign Paul!" the announcer introduced me.

I could hear clear chatter over the intercom, and it made me nervous. Truth squeezed my hand as he looked over to me and nodded his head. I gave him one last look, then made my way to the stage. Truth gave me the confidence I needed, and like I said, I trusted his judgment.

The lights in the arena went black, and the moment I took my seat, a purple light came on, and the makeshift rain began to fall from the ceiling. The beat dropped, and when it was time for me to begin singing, I looked into the crowd and captured everyone's attention.

"I never meant to cause you any sorrow
I never meant to cause you any pain
I only wanted to one time to see you laughing
I only wanted to see you
Laughing in the purple rain!"

I sang my heart out to Prince's "Purple Rain" with tears pouring down my face. Thank God for the rain because my tears blended right in, and it was perfect. I continued to sing as I looked over to Truth. He was smiling hard, but his eyes held sentiment. It was like he knew I was singing to him, and I was. One thing I never meant to do was hurt him or ever cause any pain. This man was my world, and I prayed he heard me loud and clear through the lyrics of this song.

"I never wanted to be your weekend lover
I only wanted to be some kind of friend (hey)
Baby, I could never steal you from another
It's such a shame our friendship had to end..."

I assumed I was doing great because the crowd had stood to their feet and got in tune with me. This made me feel good, and I knew after today, I was back. Everything at this moment was perfect and the only thing I was missing was Oshey. I chose not to let her continue being my Publicist because she was the one who had helped fuck my life up. When I told Truth who had got me addicted, it was like she fell off the face of the earth.

I stopped singing and began playing my guitar with so much force. I didn't know why, but something pulled my attention, and when I looked over, Raylen was backstage with Serenity nestled in her arms. Just seeing my daughter made my heart melt. It was like my emotions began to get the best of me, because I dropped to my knees, and my guitar went crashing into the ground.

The crowd erupted, and the entire front row was in tears. I looked over to Raylen, as I was breathing hard, nearly out of breath, but I wasn't tired. I was overwhelmed. I lay my body completely down onto the stage and let the rain cover me. Suddenly, I felt the presence of Truth, and it made me look up. He grabbed my hand and slowly pulled me to my feet. We stood there for a few moments, and everything around me began to spin.

I swear it felt like something out of a movie. He pulled me closely into him, and out of nowhere, he kissed me so passionately the crowd let out a warming, "Awwwe." My body began shaking, and my adrenaline began racing throughout my body. The interview with Lue crossed my mind, and the way I declined our relationship played through my mind. This was the time I redeemed myself, so I built up all the confidence I had in the world.

I wrapped my arms around him tightly and accepted his

kiss. I kissed him with so much force everyone began laughing. When we broke our kiss, I looked over to Raylen, and her smile lit up the room. I smiled at her shyly until it registered; Serenity. I ran over and took her into my arms. I walked back onto the stage and stood next to Truth. He placed a gentle kiss on Serenity's cheek, and again, the crowd was touched.

This was the perfect ending to a storm, but a new beginning to not only a fresh start in my career, but a love that I wouldn't take for granted. I loved this man with all my heart, and with God allowing me a second chance, I wasn't gonna fuck it up.

"I love you, Truth."

"I love you too, Reign Paul."

THE END!!!!

Visit My Website
http://authorbrbiescott.com/?v=7516fd43adaa
Barbie Scott Book Trap
https://www.facebook.com/
groups/1624522544463985/
Like My Page On Facebook
https://www.facebook.com/
AuthorBarbieScott/?modal=composer
Instagram:
https://www.instagram.com/authorbarbiescott